CANCER

'Could I ask yo[...]

'Uh-oh. Of course; a[...]

'I still can't understand why your circumstances have to be such a deadly secret. Why
did you tell *me*?'

'If you remember, when we first met you stated
quite categorically that a husband and children
were not on the horizon for you.'

'So you felt you were safe from—what did you
call it—offers of emotional and physical
comfort, did you? I don't know if I am flattered
or insulted.'

Christine Adams is a registered nurse, living in the West Country, who has worked for many years in the National Health Service and still nurses part-time. She has been writing for the past ten years, mainly short stories and articles. She finds the drama and tensions in the medical world an ideal background in which to find plots and storylines.

Recent titles by the same author:

SMOOTH OPERATOR
TROUBLED HEARTS
LOVE BLOOMS
DEMPSEY'S DILEMMA

EMERGENCY

BY
CHRISTINE ADAMS

MILLS & BOON®

All the characters in this book have no existence outside the imagination of the author, and have no relation whatsoever to anyone bearing the same name or names. They are not even distantly inspired by any individual known or unknown to the author, and all the incidents are pure invention.

*First published in Great Britain 1998
Harlequin Mills & Boon Limited,
Eton House, 18-24 Paradise Road, Richmond, Surrey TW9 1SR*

© Christine Adams 1998

ISBN 0 263 81244 8

*Set in Times Roman 11 on 12 pt.
03-9811-44062-D*

*Printed and bound in Norway
by AiT Trondheim AS, Trondheim*

CHAPTER ONE

SHERRIE'S head jerked upright as the noise of the emergency phone shrilled through the accident department, dragging her abruptly from her sleep. She glanced up at the clock on the wall opposite.

'Three a.m.,' she groaned. Just the time when the body was at its lowest ebb. At least she'd managed to snatch a couple of hours' doze after her continuous fourteen hours on duty.

Her eyes gritty and her mouth dry, she pulled herself unwillingly from the office armchair. She pushed her arms into the sleeves of her starched white coat and, gathering stethoscope, pens and torch from the desk, stowed them in her pockets.

She stumbled to the wash-basin in the corner of the room to splash her face, grimacing in the mirror at the tangled mass of coppery hair which had slipped from its clips during the night. Raking her fingers through it to try to bring about some semblance of order, she hurried towards the reception area to see just what the emergency phone call had been about.

'What is it, Kate?' she muttered as she reached the staff nurse, whose night-duty pallor reflected her own fatigue.

'Road traffic accident. Motorbike in collision with a car. Rider and pillion passenger hurt. Don't know the extent of the injuries yet,' the other girl said quietly, pushing an instrument trolley through the doors into the resuscitation cubicle.

'And there's a fifteen-year-old, a paracetamol over-dose, just arrived. I've bleeped the anaesthetist to put a tube down to protect the airway while we do the wash-out. Some night, eh, Sherrie?' she called over her shoulder.

'At midnight I thought we'd never get the place cleared. The only good thing—at night we haven't got all the hammering from the building work to get on our nerves.'

'A paracetamol overdose at this hour? How long ago did she take them? Has she had a wash-out? Here we go again,' Sherrie said desperately as she took ampoules from the drug cupboard and laid them out neatly beside syringes of differing sizes. 'And to think I was cock-a-hoop when I knew I'd got this job. Even though I was a last-minute choice with a very scrappy interview.'

'Don't you like it here, then?'

'Of course I do. I love the challenge and the vari-ety. I'm just having a moan. I didn't know then the stress and lack of sleep were going to age me a hun-dred years in a few days.' She rubbed her hands im-patiently over her face. 'What a sight!'

'Don't be daft.' The other girl grinned. 'Apart from your hair not being in its usual sophisticated roll, you look fine. To tell you the truth, it's quite sexy, all disarrayed like that.' She paused as she straightened the sheets on the stretcher. 'Perhaps the workload might be more organised when the new consultant gets going.'

'When will that be?'

'Dunno know for sure. He's arrived at the hospital but isn't yet in full swing. Haven't you seen him yet?' Kate gave an extravagant sigh. 'He's gorgeous— Heathcliff with a twinkle in his eyes.'

'You must have studied him hard and long.'

'There'll be a few hearts broken, I reckon.'

'Not mine, for sure. I had to work so hard to get through med school, and I'm not about to waste all those years of study, going dreamy-eyed over the local heartthrob.' And there is no way I could let Dad down. She yawned, a flush staining her high cheekbones. Silently the two women worked side by side.

'Will either of the RTA patients need a tube down, do you think?'

Kate frowned. 'Might do if there's a neck injury. As long as he or she is breathing OK the paramedics will leave the doubtful pleasure of passing a tube into the windpipe for you or for an anaesthetist to deal with when they get here. As far as I know, they've just done basic resuscitation—got a good sinus rhythm, with the heartbeat steady, and stopped the worst of the bleeding.'

Sherrie shook her head. 'I don't know how they can manage to do all that while they are avoiding other traffic, with the ambulance careering through the streets. I can barely manage to intubate with everything as steady as a rock and the patient completely still on the stretcher.'

'They do get loads of practice, and you've only been here a week or so, Doctor,' Kate reassured her.

'Still sounds funny to be called that.'

Kate glanced at her watch. 'If we shift we might just have time for a very quick coffee.'

'Don't disappear completely, will you? It's still good to have some moral support.'

'I'm only next door. At least we've got all the small cases clear so we should be able to concentrate on this patient without interruption and not have to worry about suturing cuts, bloody noses, sprained ankles and any other minor injuries waiting.'

'Apart from the overdose,' Sherrie reminded her.

Impatiently, she looked at the clock.

'They're taking their time, aren't they? I'd better see the overdose in the meantime.' She took the treatment card and walked swiftly to the cubicle indicated by Kate. Rob, the charge nurse, and another nurse were already there, and glanced up at her approach. A tall man with dark hair cut close to his head eyed her steadily for a moment before he bent over the unconscious patient, pushing aside the tangled mass of thick blonde hair on the pillow.

'Are you Jackie's mother?' Sherrie put an arm around the shoulders of an anxious-looking woman, fidgeting nervously with the frill of a pink nightdress visible below the hem of her coat, who nodded.

'Do you know how long ago she took the tablets?' the tall man said quietly.

'Who's he?' Sherrie muttered to Rob from the corner of her mouth as she examined Jackie, checking the level of consciousness.

'Sorry, do you mean me?' Brilliant blue eyes stared intently at Sherrie as the stranger pulled off his face mask, revealing a smile that brought an unexpected flutter to her heart.

'I'm sorry not to have introduced myself. We haven't met before, have we? I'm Tim O'Neill, the new consultant.' He thrust out his hand and Sherrie winced at its firm grip.

'You've got very good hearing, haven't you?'

He nodded, a mischievous twinkle just apparent in the depths of those cobalt blue eyes.

'Yes, and very useful it is, too, at times.'

'What are you doing here in the middle of the night?'

'I'm observing all the stages of emergency care, from the first pick-up of accident victims right through to the final ward admission.'

'Fancy being here from choice when you could be tucked up in bed at home. Have you finished? If so, could I examine Jackie and get her to the ward?'

'Sorry. I can see I'm in the way.' Tim moved away from the trolley with a bow. 'It's all yours, Miss or is it Ms—?'

'I'm usually known by my first name.'

'And that is.'

'Sherrie.'

'Unusual,' he murmured softly. 'A perfect match for the colour of your eyes.'

Blushing deeply, Sherrie took the medical forms from Rob, who was listening to the quiet conversation with interest.

'Women's Medical has a bed available for Jackie,' he said with a smile.

'Good. I'll finish the rest of her notes in a minute. Where's that RTA, Rob? It's taking its time, isn't it?'

'Sounds like the ambulance now.' He pushed the trolley into the corner and led the way to the main entrance, where the noise of a stretcher as it bumped against the swing doors announced the latest arrival.

Walking calmly but swiftly, two paramedics pushed the trolley. The patient was a middle-aged man, grey-faced and sweating. Dark blood stains were visible on his denim-covered legs and his rapid breathing was clearly audible through a white plastic mask.

'No tube, then,' Sherrie muttered to one of the two men as he steadied an infusion bottle on the supporting pole.

'No, he got too distressed at the idea and was managing to breathe quite well on his own so we were advised by base to leave it,' he explained quietly. 'And his heart rate went haywire when we tried, anyway.' He indicated the small portable monitor, with its zigzag lines running across the screen, as they went quickly into the cubicle and lined up the stretcher with the ease of long familiarity.

By this time the team, led by Tim, had arrived at the resuscitation area. He nodded reassuringly at everyone as, like some bizarre ballet, the staff surrounded the patient and moved into place.

Sherrie hurried to collect drugs to sedate and relax her patient.

'Are you going to intubate him?' Kate whispered.

'I think I'd better leave it to Dr O'Neill to decide. Let's see what the blood oxygen levels are. Can you get a blood gas reading for me, please?' She pulled her mask into place and snapped on latex gloves. 'He looks pretty grey and his oxygen saturation could be better,' she continued, looking at the small dial that registered oxygen figures.

'Try to relax, Mr Reynolds,' Sherrie reassured the anxious man. 'I'm Sherrie Walker, the casualty officer. Do you mind if I call you by your first name?'

'Not at all.' He moved his head very slightly from side to side, the large surgical collar obviously rubbing against his chin, his wispy grey hair stuck to the side of his head.

'Where is the worst pain, John? In your hip and thigh?' she asked as he nervously clasped her hand. Wide-eyed, he watched as Kate, with large shears, cut rapidly at the side seam of his jeans.

'I will be all right, won't I, Doctor?' he muttered hoarsely. 'Won't I?'

'Of course. Now, take it easy.' Gently Sherrie released her hand. 'We'll get you sorted out and comfortable as quickly as we can.'

In an aside, she said, 'Kate, let's catheterise and see if there is any blood in the urine. Then X-rays of his pelvis and chest and neck.' She scribbled busily on the treatment card.

Kate glanced up, carefully edging the heavy denim material away from the injured limb.

'Where's my wife?' John Reynolds moved his head against the pillows.

'She's fine—in the other cubicle,' Sherrie said, glancing through the glass screen. 'X-rays of pelvis and chest, please. What do you think, Dr O'Neill?'

The consultant, who'd be silently watching, moved

to the side of the stretcher, his hands clasped in front of him.

'Yes. May I?' He began to examine the patient, carefully compressing the side of Mr Reynolds's hips and then feeling gently down the left thigh.

'Sorry, have I missed something?'

Tim shook his head. 'No, a perfect examination,' he said.

'X-ray is ready.' Rob waved from the doorway to attract her attention.

'Good,' Sherrie said firmly. 'Let's get this poor man down there so that we can see the extent of the damage.'

'How about some morphine before we start to pull him about?' Tim took the end of the stretcher.

'If there hadn't been so many interruptions, I would have given some by now,' Sherrie said through gritted teeth to Kate. She turned away. 'Twenty milligrams, please.'

'And a first dose for a tetanus course?' Tim's smile was mischievous.

'It's written up. I don't know about you,' she said, looking stiffly up at Tim, 'but I think it's one of the most irritating things in the world to be told what to do when you're just about to do it anyway. I'll come down to X-ray, Rob.'

'Sure.' Rob quickly gave the two injections as the little cavalcade went towards the lifts. The doors were about to close as Sherrie glanced over her shoulder at the watching consultant.

'Thank you for all your help, Dr O'Neill,' she called softly, in a voice as sweet as honey, 'but I think we can manage now.' A grin spread cross her face at his frown and the lift doors clanged shut behind her before he could reply.

'That made you feel better, did it?' Rob winked.

'Childish of me, I know, but he is high-handed, isn't he? Well, not high-handed exactly but he's the consultant and let's you know it. And a bit patronising. Perhaps I'm rather defensive because I hate someone looking over my shoulder when I'm working, especially being a mere female!'

'He has a very good reputation, on the ball and innovative, though at the same time prepared to listen to constructive criticism. Do you get much trouble because of your sex? Professionally speaking, of course.' Rob's grey eyes crinkled at Sherrie's frown.

'Not usually. In fact, I've come across very little sexual prejudice.'

'Luckier than me, then. Why say "male nurse",' Rob said gloomily. 'They don't say "female nurse", do they? Still, attitudes are improving.'

'We'll be able to cry on one another's shoulders if it gets to be too much for us.' Sherrie laughed softly, tilting her head towards him.

'If what gets too much for you?' Sherrie turned on her heel at the sound of Tim's voice at the entrance to X-Ray as the porters and technicians brought in Mr Reynolds.

'Oh, nothing important,' she said hastily. Lucky I wasn't talking about him just then, she thought.

'Are these temporary splints firm enough for us to move him to the X-ray table?' asked one of the porters.

'If I give a little more analgesia it should be all right.'

Quickly Sherrie took the syringe from the tray and neatly injected a small amount of drug into John Reynolds's vein, trying hard to ignore Tim's gaze. But it was no good. He did make her nervous, which was unusual. Normally, she prided herself on the confident face she presented to the patients and other staff. The staff vacated the X-ray area as the radiologist started the machine.

'Deep breath—hold it—right,' she called. Minutes later, the X-ray films were complete and the entourage left the department and returned to Casualty. Sherrie went to the X-ray display screen and studied the first of the films, standing at Tim's shoulder.

'They don't look too bad.' She gazed intently.

'Hmm. We'd better get the orthopaedic team to see them, all the same.' Tim pulled thoughtfully at his lower lip. 'The cervical and thoracic spine are OK but down here...' he shuffled the films '...there's a nasty crack in the pelvis—there. Can you see it?'

'I don't know if the orthopaedics will want to try and pin it tonight—or this morning, rather.' He glanced down at his watch. 'But I think sooner rather than later would be better, and perhaps pin the femur as well. I'll see what the registrar says.' He turned and looked at Sherrie. 'What about Mrs Reynolds?'

'Superficial injuries only. She could go home, but obviously she doesn't want to leave until she knows about her husband.'

'I'll leave that to you, then.' He strode out, letting the doors swing to behind him.

'Well, that was more straightforward than I thought it was going to be,' Sherrie said with a sigh as they all sat in the office. 'I'm glad Mr Reynolds hasn't done any damage to his spine. How is his wife? Is she quite comfortable? I'll take some blood specimens and also I could get some cross-matched in case Mr Reynolds needs transfusing later. Judging by the swelling around the fracture of his thigh, I should think he must have bled loads into the muscle there.'

Massaging her aching back as she stood, Sherrie picked up the notes and went to the treatment area, collecting syringes and specimen tubes on the way.

'Anything else you want a hand with?'

Sherrie shook her head as Tim appeared in the doorway.

'No, I think I've finished now, thank you, Dr O'Neill.'

'For heaven's sake, call me Tim.' He flicked her cheek lightly with his finger. He studied her through half-closed eyes, but even then their vivid colour could be clearly seen. 'You've done well tonight.'

'I enjoy being busy, but thanks for those few kind words, anyway,' she said huskily, unexpectedly stirred by the feather-light touch of his hand against her skin.

'How come I didn't see you at your interview?'

'You were away at a conference. The original candidate was taken ill and had to pull out. I was second choice, but was asked to start more or less straight away.' She pushed her hair back impatiently. 'I was very glad to do so before I forgot all I'd learnt in medical school.'

'Don't think that will happen. You'll find it all gets set more firmly in your mind as you deal with more and more cases that match the textbooks. I'm off now. No doubt I'll see you during today some time.'

He went through the outer doors with a wave as Sherrie returned to the main department area, picking out fresh supplies of syringes and swabs to stock the emergency trolley.

'We'll see to that,' Kate protested. 'You go and finish your coffee and relax before we get the next run of patients.'

'That would be lovely. Half past five and it's already getting light so it's not worth going back to bed. I'll just wait in the office and write up the rest of my notes until Mike takes over from me.'

Sherrie paused and breathed deeply in that fresh morning air as she stood outside the accident department. There wasn't an ambulance to be seen.

'Trust it to be so quiet for the start of Mike's shift, lucky devil. He always gets the easy shifts. Never mind, at least I'm free and it's such a lovely morning, too,' she murmured, looking at the pale yet brilliant sky and the dusting of early green shoots on the branches of the trees. What a busy shift it had been.

Even the past hour, when she'd hoped it would quieten a little, had had its excitement after Mr Reynolds's transfer to Theatre. Young Jackie, the overdose patient, had deteriorated, before going to the ward, and had had to be sent straight to Intensive Care. I only hope we got her stomach washed out in good time. Sherrie frowned to herself. Then no sooner had we started the infusion with the antidote when an ambulance had screeched to a halt—that massive heart attack. Wow! Lucky to survive.

Forget work, Sherrie told herself sharply. We got him back all right. She clutched at her stomach as it gave a demanding rumble. Golly, she couldn't remember when she'd last eaten. She glanced at her watch. It was far too early for the general cafeteria to be open. If she hurried there might be some breakfast left in the doctors' dining room and she could grab a bite, before going to bed.

But the fresh morning air was too good to waste after a night in the depths of the hospital and Sherrie turned on her heel and set out along the path that cut across the grounds.

'Good morning!'

Sherrie turned at the sound of Tim's voice as he appeared from the doorway of the theatre block. 'All finished?'

'Yes, food, coffee and bed in that order.' She grinned up at him, surprised that she hadn't noticed before what an attractive smile he had. Too much in awe of him, perhaps.

'I hope you were refreshed by your sleep in the night.'

'My sleep in the night?' Sherrie frowned.

'Yes, I had to call at the office for some paperwork, and you were out for the count.'

'Oh, no, how embarrassing. I'm sorry about that.'

'Don't be. One of the first things to learn in the medical profession is to get what sleep you can when you can. And you looked so charming I didn't have the heart to wake you, even if I'd needed to. Do you think you'll be able to stand up to the rigours of the accident department?'

'Of course. How do you mean?'

'You looked so fragile—positively ethereal, in fact.'

Sherrie nearly laughed out loud. Ethereal! he should see her at home! Three older brothers, all the teasing she could stand and she'd more than held her own in their childhood fights. His words had probably been meant as a compliment but she felt a prickle of irritation.

Once again, as in the department, she felt swamped by his obvious medical expertise, his undoubted masculinity and a feeling that she was being taken over.

With a deep breath she pushed the thought aside. As a consultant, he had every right to take over at work and sort out the priorities, and as long as she had some chance to prove herself and her ability she must just get used to his way of working.

He fell into step beside her. 'Fancy a stroll? Hardly anyone about just yet and, you must admit, it's a very pretty morning—apart from all the building work on the A and E extension.'

'That's a bit heart-breaking, isn't it, seeing all those lovely trees chopped down?'

'Unfortunately, progress has its price.'

'But it seems to me that progress always means pulling something down and, I'm sorry to say, replacing it with something inferior. Sorry, I shouldn't sound off. I'll be glad of a walk. I feel as though I've been buried in the bowels of the hospital for ever.'

She glanced up. 'You look different,' she said with a frown.

'It's these, I expect.' He lifted the tinted glasses from his nose as he moved up beside her.

'You weren't wearing them earlier, were you?' She studied the fine gold frames as Tim replaced them.

'No, I'm short-sighted so don't need them for close work.'

Sherrie sighed. If anything, the simple frames enhanced his piercing eyes. Short-sighted, she thought, hence the penetrating stare. And I thought he was overwhelmed by my feminine charms.

She stifled a giggle at the small conceit and swung happily along the path, enjoying his company and the outlook as the fingers of dawn crept across a lightening sky, which rapidly developed into pastels of all shades from faint apricot and peach to a soft yellow, eventually becoming silky lilac then blue.

Not speaking, they strolled on through the hospital grounds, where the flower-beds had a few spikes of green from brave daffodils, pushing above the surface of the ground.

'I always reckon that's one of the, if not the only, advantages of working during the night—the chance to greet the dawn, especially on a lovely spring morning like this. How are you enjoying the accident centre work? Or is it too soon to know yet? Some people love it, the constant challenge of never knowing what's coming through the door and the variety of anything from a splinter in a finger to a severe head injury or poisoning of a child.'

'I haven't really had time to get used to it, but so

far so good. The only aspect I dread is the idea of small children being injured, possibly in a car accident or, even worse, burnt.' Sherrie shivered.

'I agree, but let's not think of such unpleasant things in this.' He swept his arm in a large arc to indicate the soft green growth on the trees and the flower-beds with a few brave splashes of colour from some hardy perennials.

'My pre-registration job was in a city centre hospital in South London—all mean streets and concrete high-rise. This is like being on holiday.' She paused as they reached the perimeter fence of the hospital. 'And it's not far from home. I grew up near here. Well, I think it's shower and bed now. I've actually got forty-eight hours off, time enough to recover and have time to myself.'

'I've got a couple of patients to see, and then I'll be on my way home. I should be able to join my family for breakfast.'

'Your family?'

'Yes. Laura and my daughter, Amy. Goodnight— or good morning, rather. Enjoy your time off and I'll see you, no doubt, in the madhouse when you return.'

Self-consciously aware of his gaze following her as she walked away, Sherrie hurried back towards her room in the doctors' residence, shivering now as a breeze sprang up which cut through her white coat and the thin material of the cotton blouse and skirt. So he had a family? Why the small thread of disappointment which went through her? Hastily, she pushed the thought aside.

The smell of toast and coffee drew her to the big

self-service kitchen. At first it had been disconcerting not to have a proper dining service as in her previous hospital, but now she could see the advantages of being able to get at least a snack-style meal at any time. And, if she was lucky this morning, there might even be a few rashers of bacon about as well.

'Tough night, Sherrie?' a couple of people asked sympathetically as they passed through the breakfast area, hurrying to ward rounds and theatre lists. Sherrie nodded and took a plate. She perched on a stool in the large, sunlit room and briskly buttered a slice of overdone toast.

No one had time to stop for a gossip and Sherrie soon reached her room, her shower taking only a few minutes.

Pulling down the heavy blind in the bedroom, she scrambled into bed as quickly as possible, but as she settled her head on the pillows she suddenly felt embarrassed at the idea of Tim seeing her fast sleep in the office. I bet I had my mouth open and was snoring or, even worse, was dribbling.

But even this embarrassing idea was not enough to keep her awake for long and she drifted into dreams, haunted by racing ambulances, stretchers and a pair of piercing blue eyes.

CHAPTER TWO

'HAVE we got many booked for orthopaedic follow-up?'

Sherrie picked up the heap of white cards from the reception desk and hastily riffled through them. Originally she'd wondered if it might be rather boring, compared with the normal routine of the accident department, but now she found she didn't mind the thought of the more monotonous job of checking X-rays, plasters and physiotherapy appointments.

'It still seems funny, having to do this. I thought it was more a job for the orthopaedic team.'

'I believe that during the last meeting Tim O'Neill suggested we try it as a double safeguard to prevent any patients slipping through the net and not getting the follow-up they need. Sometimes, after a really frantic day and night, there can be as many as fifty follow-ups.'

'Let's hope there aren't as many as that today,' Sherrie groaned. 'I want to get away this afternoon. One thing about doing the clinic—at least the working day should be shorter. Hark at me! This is the doctor who is prepared to give up all for her career.'

'Going somewhere special?' Rob grinned as they went to collect the sheaf of notes and X-rays.

'Not really. Well, I suppose it is. It's my sister-in-law's birthday, and we're having a family get-together and then a big party for her on Saturday. If she lasts that long. She's very pregnant.'

'Well, there shouldn't be any problems about getting away, should there?'

'As long as that wretch, Mike, turns up in time to take over. Did you know he overslept the other day and I didn't get away till nearly eleven? Bit much after being on all night.'

'It won't affect you with the clinic, anyway. He was here bright and early. Very early, in fact. We had an accidental poisoning so he was called at six. Though how anyone could call twenty paracetamol accidental, I don't know. Silly little madam of fourteen had a row with her boyfriend, and it was only when her father went to call her that he found her.

'God knows how much liver damage she'll have suffered in that time. We gave her the parvolex, even though it might have been a bit late.'

'The what?' Sherrie queried, listening with only half an ear.

'Parvolex, the antidote. As it is, I think she'll have to be transferred to a specialist unit. Several liver function tests were abnormal. Couldn't you just shake them sometimes? Doesn't she care what her parents are going through?'

'I suppose it doesn't seem serious to just swallow a few headache pills. If they only knew how the damage goes on afterwards. And that's the second one in less than a week.' Sherrie shook her head. 'Anyway, I'll get on with the clinic. Will Tim O'Neill be sitting in on this as well?'

'Not the clinic. The orthopaedic registrar, Matt Sefton, is coming.'

Sherrie stifled momentary disappointment at the thought that she wouldn't be working with Tim. Despite her original awe of him, she was beginning to appreciate his complete calm, whatever the emergency, and an underlying quirky humour that appealed to her sense of the ridiculous.

There was a developing closeness between them, though on the surface he'd been no more than professional, even slightly impatient if he thought any care was not as it should be.

'I'd better make a move. Judging by the look of these appointment cards, we've got more than enough follow-ups here.'

'See you around, Sherrie. Who's on tomorrow?'

'Me, for my sins. Hope it's not too busy. I've got some papers I want to rewrite during this week.'

The morning passed in a flurry of appointments and assessments, mostly fractured wrists and some whiplash neck injuries. Generally, the injured were making good progress, and Sherrie felt confident enough to order the follow-up X-rays and physiotherapy appointments. Matt, a quiet, fair-haired man with glasses, also increased her feelings of confidence as he confirmed most of her assessments.

'Hello, Simon, how's that wrist of yours?' Sherrie smiled at the young boy, just coming through the door. He smiled shyly and happily accepted her examination.

'Mmm,' she reassured his mother. 'Fingers and

pulse all good. Has there been any pain to worry him?'

'No, only if he forgets and moves a bit awkwardly.'

'That's good. We'll see you in a couple of weeks. Don't forget to keep those fingers wriggling, will you? Are you back at school? The next time I see you I shall expect to see a lot of autographs on that plaster.' He smiled and hurried out.

Immersed in the busyness of the morning, Sherrie had no idea of the time and she was shocked when she realised it was already one-thirty.

'Anything else?' she asked Rob, 'or can I get away now?'

'I'm sure it's OK. Just look how quiet it is out there.' He pointed to the general work area where only one patient sat, waiting.

'God, Mike must have shifted to get everything as straight as this.'

'Actually, Tim has been here as well. Talk about a human dynamo—in the nicest way, of course.' As if the mention of his name had conjured him up, Tim appeared from his office.

'Morning.' He nodded, the tails of his white coat flying out behind him, his distinctive walk almost a prowl as he disappeared towards the lift.

'Sorry I wasn't here to see it all happening. But I'm going. I've left my telephone number just in case. I told Tim I would, though he said not to worry. Tell Mike I'll see him at change-over Thursday morning.'

She slipped off her white coat and gathered her bag from the office, then hurried out to her Mini, parked behind the department, swearing under her breath at the layers of dust across the top from the nearby building work.

My own fault, she thought. Shouldn't have left it here.

Throwing her bag onto the back seat, she started the engine and set off towards the main drive, shutting her mind to the fifteen-mile-an-hour speed limit in the hospital grounds before she reached the gate and set off for home.

'I'm home, Mum,' Sherrie called as she opened the front door of the sprawling house, pleasantly rural despite the housing estate creeping up around it and a small factory nearby. Built of cream-coloured stone, her parents had lived there since their marriage, and John Walker still ran his general practice surgery from the small extension at the side.

She still called it home, even after all her time away at university, and even kept some clothes and other belongings there. Her mother appeared from the kitchen at the back of the hall, a rich baking aroma wafting out at the same time.

'You're in good time. Have you had something to eat?' Her mother kissed her warmly on the cheek. 'You look tired.'

'No, I haven't and I'd love some lunch, thanks, and, yes, I am a bit weary. Where's Dad?'

'He's just been called out. Do you remember old Mrs Simmonds?'

'Good grief, Mum, is she still alive? She must be ninety at least.'

'Ninety-five and as sharp as two pins, but she's had a cough which has hung on longer than your dad likes so he's gone to check on her. But we can still have something.'

'He must be the only GP in the country who still runs the practice in the old way, with the GP being on call.'

'You know you'll never change him and he's happier, working that way. But I've actually persuaded him to take a break, said I needed it, and I've got a locum. How about that? She may be looking in later so you'll get a chance to meet her.'

'That must have taken some doing. Talking of being on call, I left this number—I hope you don't mind—in case they need me at the hospital.'

Her mother ran impatient fingers through her hair.

'Not another one,' she groaned.

'It's all right. The chances of being called are so remote as to be hardly worth considering. I'll just change and be with you straight away.' She ran lightly up the stairs to 'her' room and quickly washed and pulled on an old sweatshirt and jeans, before returning to the big farmhouse-style kitchen.

'Actually, I'm not sorry your father isn't here. I'll get a chance to talk to you about everyday family matters before the conversation becomes swamped in medicine.'

There was a splutter as Mrs Walker tipped the beaten eggs into a pan onto the lightly fried mushrooms then moments later turned the fluffy omelette onto a plate. 'Here you are. Salad in the bowl, bread and butter on the side and I've just made a fresh pot of tea.'

'Gosh, this looks good. I don't know how you always manage to get the omelette to rise so much. I do exactly the same as you, but with me the omelette has as much depth as a pancake.'

'Fresh eggs and lots of beating and cook very quickly.' Her mother smiled, obviously pleased at the compliment.

'Aren't you joining me?' Sherrie picked up her fork and tucked in hungrily.

'I'll wait for Dad.'

'How are the preparations going for Saturday? I hope you're not trying to do everything yourself,' Sherrie said sternly. 'I wish I could do more, but—'

'I'm doing very little, I promise. David and Caroline are organising it all.'

'I'll believe that when I see it. And how's my gorgeous nephew?'

'He's absolutely beautiful. Getting rather spoilt. He has David's eyes exactly at that age and the same wicked look about him. And he's so knowing—you can barely believe he's only four. When you've finished eating I'll show you the latest photographs.'

Sherrie mopped up the last of the juices with her bread and sighed. 'That was delicious, Mum.'

'Anything else? Home-made fruit cake?'

'Nothing else, just another cup of tea. It's all right, I'll pour it—you get those photos.' Sherrie refilled the cups then took the wallet and shook out the snaps. 'You're right, Mum, even though you're his grandmother and likely to be prejudiced you're right in this case. He looks adorable.' She picked over the photos, studying them intently, and felt an unexpected yearning at the sight of the smiling face of her nephew.

'Anyway, no need to look at photographs—they're coming over this afternoon and you can see him in the flesh.'

Her mother took the envelope and placed it on the sideboard, before clearing the dishes away.

'Let me give you a hand with the washing-up.'

'That's all right. I'll leave the dishes until after your father has had his lunch.' She glanced at the clock. 'He shouldn't be much longer now. You go and sit down and have a glance at the paper.'

'All right, if you're sure. It has been pretty busy lately.' Sherrie sighed gratefully as she sank back against the cushioning of the old-fashioned armchair in the corner. 'I love this kitchen.' She looked at the Aga cooker and polished wood shelves. 'I always think it's what a kitchen should be.'

'You're right.' Both women jumped at the sound of the voice from the doorway as John Walker appeared.

'I didn't hear your car arrive.'

Sherrie's father smiled. 'I didn't intend you to. I wanted to surprise you both. I thought I might hear something interesting.' He kissed his wife briefly on the cheek and hugged Sherrie as she scrambled from the chair.

'Want to sit here, Dad?'

'No, I'm all ready for some lunch. I expect you are, too.'

'Hope you don't mind. I sneaked in ahead. Mum, as usual, thought I looked as though I needed immediate nourishment.'

'Well, you do look a pit peaky.' Her father gazed fondly at her. 'Not working you too hard, are they?'

'No more than I can handle. How about you?'

Sherrie tried to stifle the momentary dismay she felt at the sight of her father's drawn face. He had shadows beneath his eyes and his skin looked grey in the unflattering light of the fluorescent tube as he hung his jacket over the back of the chair and pulled impatiently at his tie.

'Well, pretty busy. The flu outbreak hasn't helped, I must admit. The good old cliché, "there's a lot of it about," couldn't be more true. Never mind, I think we're coming to the end of it now. Has your mother told you she's blackmailed me into taking a break?'

'And a good thing, too.'

'Enough of me. How's Dr Walker, junior?'

'I'm enjoying it now that I'm gaining a bit of confidence. Our consultant is very good and guides us well. You could imagine him dealing with any sort of emergency, such as a major alert, as well as all the day-to-day running of the department. I wouldn't want to cross him, though. He can sound a bit impatient sometimes and I don't think he would suffer fools gladly.'

'Is he married?' Mrs Walker cut in abruptly.

'Well, I assume so. He has a daughter, anyway. Some of the long-term staff have welcomed him with open arms because he's managing to get lots of improvements done with the actual building and so forth.'

'What did you say his name was? I know you told

me but I've forgotten. One of the penalties of old age, I suppose.'

'Tim O'Neill. Did you ever come across him?'

'No, different generation.' Her father picked up his knife and fork and looked hungrily at his plate.

'I'll shut up while you get on with your lunch, Dad. We can have a proper chinwag after you've eaten.'

'I want to know all the up-to-date happenings, mind. Saves me the bother of reading the medical journals.'

There was silence, apart from the ticking of the big old clock on the dresser, as Sherrie's parents ate their lunch and she flicked lazily through the local paper.

'Uh-oh, more protests at the new bypass,' she murmured. 'You can understand both points of view, but the violence is surely unnecessary. Have you finished eating? If so, I'll make some coffee, shall I?'

'It's already percolating. I remembered that, unlike Dad and me, you prefer it to tea.'

'Bet you got it especially for me, didn't you?'

'Not at all. David and Caroline will be here soon and I expect they'll be glad of a cup.' She stood and sliced the large rich fruit cake in the centre of the table as the front door opened. There was a scampering of footsteps in the hall and Sherrie's nephew catapulted through the door, followed more sedately by his parents.

'Granma, Gramps, we're going to the park this afternoon. There's a fair and Daddy said as well as going on the swings I can have a ride on the car-car...' He paused and looked up hopefully.

'On the carousel.'

Sherrie's sister-in-law gave a grateful sigh as she sank onto a chair and smoothed a hand over her enlarged stomach.

'It's got to be another boy the way he's kicking.'

'I've got coffee made.' Mrs Walker pushed back her chair, 'or would you rather have something else to drink?'

'Coffee would be lovely. I allow myself two cups a day.' Caroline smiled.

In the ensuing babble of voices Sherrie studied her father surreptiously. Having rested and eaten, he looked much better. Perhaps it was just tiredness, as he'd said.

'We must get on with discussing this party on Saturday.' Mrs Walker drained her cup and placed it firmly on the table.

'Would you be very disappointed if we kept it just to the family do tonight, Mum?' David asked anxiously. 'You'll go overboard as always.' He laughed. 'And I think anything else would be too much for Caroline at the moment, anyway.'

'I do get pretty tired,' she said apologetically. 'And don't forget—Ben was early.'

'With two doctors there, that wouldn't be too much of a problem.'

David bent and kissed his wife's cheek. 'Oh, that's probably for me.' He hurried to the phone's peremptory summons. 'I left instructions I was to be called if they had any problems at the office.'

'Does none of my family take a break?' Mrs Walker complained as David's voice rumbled into a lengthy conversation.

He popped his head round the door shortly after. 'Sorry, folks. I'll have to get back to the office for a bit.'

'What about the F-A-I-R?' his wife spelt out.

'Sorry, I'll be back as soon as I can.'

'Don't worry, I'll take Ben.'

'Are you sure, Sherrie?'

'Of course, I'd love it. Just let me finish my coffee. You sit there and rest, Caroline, and Mum and Dad can have a quiet afternoon together for a change.

'Come on, Ben, you and I are going to the fair. Put your coat back on and I'll get my jacket. Mummy can have a rest with Granma and Gramps while you and I have all the fun.'

With her denim jacket slung over her shoulders, Sherrie zipped up Ben's anorak. Kissing his grand-parents and mother, he skipped happily along the drive and the short distance to the park. They could hear the music as they approached and streams of people went ahead of them through the gate.

'Now, listen, Ben. You must hold my hand all the time, do you understand?' Sherrie crouched in front of her nephew. 'It would be easy to get lost here with all these people, wouldn't it?'

He nodded solemnly, his blue eyes wide, then pulled her towards the organ music of what was to him the biggest attraction—the gaily painted carousel with its coloured horses.

'We'll have to wait until the next turn. Shall we wander round and see what else there is?'

'No, I stay here.' Lovingly, he rubbed his head against her sleeve, but Sherrie could see by the look of determination on his face that his red wellingtons might as well have been glued to the ground. After a few minutes the carousel stopped.

'Come on, then, our turn now.' Swiftly Sherrie helped Ben up the steps and picked the first vacant horse.

'I want the blue one.' He pointed to the horse behind.

'Sorry, Ben, that little girl is there. We'll have to take this one.'

His bottom lip quivered and then, to Sherrie's horror, he let out a shriek which could be heard above most of the various fairground noises.

'Oh, no, you don't, young man.' Holding him firmly in her arms, Sherrie struggled back down the steps.

'You look as though you're having a problem there, Dr Walker.'

Sherrie glanced up at the tall figure beside her. 'Dr O'Neill, a pleasant surprise. Let me introduce my nephew, Ben—a very disgruntled nephew at the moment.'

She set Ben down and glanced at Tim. Completely relaxed in jeans and casual shirt, he rested one shoulder against the wall of the cash desk.

Mr Cool, she thought as she struggled to push her hair back from her face and tuck her sweatshirt into her jeans, not like me.

'What's upset Ben?' He quirked an eyebrow.

'He wants that horse there, with the little girl aboard.'

'That little girl is my daughter, Amy. You can have that horse if you wish. I don't think she minds.'

'Your daughter? She's much younger than I'd pictured.' Sherrie took a deep breath, her head whirling as though she'd already been on a fast roundabout. 'That's kind of you. But, I'm sorry, he can't get away with such bad behaviour. Now, Ben, do you want to go on the carousel?'

He nodded.

'Right, it is up to you. You go on whichever horse is empty or we don't go at all.'

He gazed at her defiantly for a few seconds then, with a long, shuddering sigh, clambered back up the steps and allowed himself to be lifted onto a horse. Carefully, Sherrie scrambled up behind Ben and put an arm around his middle as the music started and the carousel began to revolve.

She turned awkwardly to wave to Tim but he'd disappeared from view. Then she saw him on the horse with his daughter, his long legs stretched out on either side.

'All right, Ben?' Sherrie murmured in the little boy's ear, firmly gripping the upright support pole.

He nodded happily, his tantrum forgotten, his face wreathed in a contented smile as the horses began their slow progression, rising and dipping in time to the music.

She leaned back and let her body sway in time to the music of the nearby hurdy-gurdy machine. All too soon for Ben the ride was over, but Sherrie was happy enough to lift him down from the shiny saddle, her legs aching from her tight grip.

'I want to go again.' Ben pulled impatiently at her hand.

'Perhaps later. But first there are lots of other things to see and to go on.'

'Do you mind if we come with you?' asked Tim, who joined them at that moment.

'No, it will be lovely to have the company. It looks as though Amy and Ben aren't averse to the idea, anyway.' Sherrie indicated the two small figures, hand-in-hand, just in front, one dark head and one blond bobbing as they chattered on happily. 'Ben, don't forget, you stay right by me. We wouldn't want you to get lost.'

'How old is your nephew?'

'Four and a bit, but rather spoilt and completely fearless. What about Amy?'

'She's five. I don't see nearly enough of her so, as I have a couple of hours free this afternoon, I thought I would grab the opportunity of having her to myself and also give Laura a break.'

'Laura?'

'Yes, my partner.'

'Your…er…partner?' The words trickled uncertainly from Sherrie's mouth. 'Sorry, what was that? You said Amy is five, didn't you? Are you sure you want to tag along with Ben and me?'

'Of course.' Tim took her arm and steered Sherrie past a patch of slippery mud.

'Thank you. She's going to break hearts some day.' A lot like her father, Sherrie thought. 'She's a little beauty.'

'Well, I think so. But, then, I'm prejudiced, of

course. What about you? No plans for marriage and children on the horizon?'

Fiercely, Sherrie shook her head. 'No, after the struggle and hard work I put into my training, I shan't be thinking of any such thing for a long time.'

'Unless the only man in the world for you appears, of course, like a bolt from the blue.'

'If he hasn't already done so.' Sherrie laughed.

'Ooh, someone at work? Are you blushing? I'm intrigued.' He smiled at her. 'Nothing to say? It's all right, I shan't pester you any more. I'll mind my own business. He could come along, and you could still continue to work.'

'Even so.'

'So you intend to keep your emotions firmly battened down.'

'If I can.' Sherrie shrugged.

Tim hurried and drew alongside the two children. 'Hey, you two, how about some popcorn?' Two small heads swivelled towards him and they proceeded along a narrow path past a Punch and Judy show, the dodgems, a guess-your-weight machine and two smaller roundabouts until finally a sweet smell drew them to a stall which sold toffee-apples and freshly made popcorn.

'Popcorn or ice creams are all right…' Sherrie lifted Ben onto a nearby park seat '…but, please, no candyfloss. I can remember getting some caught in my hair once as a child and I think Ben's mother wouldn't be very impressed with me if I took her precious son home with a pink, sticky head.'

'I can just see you as a little girl, with pink candy-floss in your hair.'

He went to the stall and bought four cone-shaped bags of popcorn, then they sat in companionable silence except for the crunching of the corn and an occasional giggle from the two little ones.

Sherrie studied Tim from the corner of her eye. At work he was almost robot-like in his efficiency and seemed to see what was going on everywhere in the department at the same time, but now he appeared completely relaxed as he leaned back, tossing the popcorn into his mouth.

'Right, my treat now.' Sherrie jumped to her feet. 'How about another ride on the roundabout?'

'Yes, please.' Clapping their hands and jumping up and down, Ben and Amy clung to her legs.

'I was about to challenge you to a duel on the dodgems, but it looks as though I'm outnumbered,' Tim said. 'Perhaps some other time. I think I might manage to hang on for one more round of the carousel, if I must.' He laughed at her across the children's heads then swung Amy into his arms. 'But after that I shall have to think of getting home.' He glanced at his watch. 'Work calls.'

'You're not going back again so soon, surely? I thought you were there for most of the morning. You know what they say about all work making Jack a dull boy.'

'So I'm dull, am I?'

'Of course not. But you soon will be at this rate.'

'I'm setting up an emergency call-out service, with medical staff on standby for the more acute emergencies, but there's still quite a lot of detail I need to sort out.'

'What—like a major alert, do you mean?' Puffing slightly to keep up with his long-legged walk and gripping Ben's hand firmly, Sherrie hurried after him.

'Rather more than that. In fact, I am having a meeting tomorrow in A and E and I shall expect all staff to be there. I've done a pretty comprehensive draft, but I'm sure there'll be a lot of comments and, hopefully, some useful points made.

'Right, Amy, Ben, here we are. One roundabout. And surprisingly empty, too.' He set Amy on the ground beside him and Sherrie lifted Ben onto the waiting carousel.

'Don't forget,' she called over her shoulder. 'My treat.'

During the time they'd been at the popcorn stall the area had filled with people, several more stalls had been set up and the noise of the crowds clashed with the various musical accompaniments. 'I think we got here just in time before it became too crowded.'

When the ride was over Sherrie carefully straightened Ben's jacket as they got down, and watched as Tim did the same to Amy. The little girl turned enormous eyes to her father and pulled him to her level to whisper in his ear.

He glanced across at Sherrie and Ben and nodded. 'I think we could arrange that. Amy would like Ben to come to tea.'

'I don't think I could answer for Ben's mother. This evening is definitely out, I'm afraid. But if you like

I'll get her to give…Laura, is it? I'll ask Caroline to ring you to arrange it.'

'And Amy wants you as well, please.'

'Oh, that would be lovely, Amy. I'll see what Ben's mummy says.' It would be interesting to see Tim at home—see another side of the man who, in spite of her best intentions, fascinated her. She smiled. 'I've enjoyed this afternoon—something different.'

'I wonder what is going on there?' Tim pointed across a narrow stretch of grass to where a group of excited figures had gathered. As they watched, a man in overalls separated from the group and raced to one of the caravans on site. Shortly after, the wail of an ambulance siren could be heard in the distance. Quickly Tim swept Amy into his arms. 'Perhaps we'd better have a look and see if we can do anything.'

'What about the children if there's been an accident? We wouldn't want them to see too much.'

Swiftly Tim put Amy down again. 'If you don't mind staying with them, I'll go and see if I can help. Amy, stay there a minute with Ben and Sherrie. Daddy won't be long.'

Sherrie took both children by the hand and wandered away in the direction of the carousel, but it was stationary and no music came from the central pillar. She glanced down as Ben tugged impatiently at her hand.

'What was that? No, I'm afraid we can't go to the fair with Amy again tomorrow, but Amy's daddy has said you can go to tea. Come on, let's see what Dr O'Neill is up to. We'd better not wander too far.'

They retraced their steps and reached the gate just

as an ambulance swerved through the entrance and towards the waiting group. Tim's tall figure was visible above the heads of the rest. Sherrie led the two children in the same direction, arriving as two paramedics closed the doors on a stretchered patient.

One of them glanced at Tim. 'You did a very efficient job, stopping the bleeding, sir. Glad to see someone is up to date with his first aid.'

Seeing Sherrie's amused expression, Tim put a warning finger to his lips and winked. The intimacy of the shared secret warmed her.

'What happened?' Sherrie asked in a quiet undertone so that the children wouldn't hear.

'One of the assistants slipped and fell under the edge of the swing boat and sustained a very nasty injury, tearing off most of the skin and calf muscle from that leg,' Tim responded softly.

'Glad to see you've kept up with your first aid,' Sherrie said, smiling mischievously. 'What you ought to do is go like blazes and get to A and E before the ambulance, all ready to greet it when they arrive.'

'That might be piling it on a bit thick.' Tim laughed. 'But I think it wouldn't be a bad idea if I went with him in the ambulance. He is bleeding badly. Would you be able to keep an eye on Amy for me?'

'Will the paramedics mind?' She glanced at them uncertainly. 'Of course I'll take Amy. I'm at my parents'. Here's the telephone number and address—pick her up when you want. Come on, Amy, would you like to come with us? Have some tea with Ben. Take his hand, there's a good girl.'

'Are you sure it's all right? I feel a bit guilty, dumping her on you like this.'

'Don't be silly. You can see Ben's thrilled to bits and I'm delighted to be able to help. Come on, young Ben, time to get home and see Mummy and Daddy.' Solemnly the two children kissed one another before Ben took Amy's hand.

'I think it must be love at first sight.' Sherrie smiled.

Did she imagine it or did Tim say 'just like her father' as he kissed Amy?

'Daddy won't be long. I've just got to make the man better. Be a good girl, won't you?' He spoke to the paramedic, then climbed swiftly into the rear of the ambulance and leaned over the injured man on the stretcher, after Sherrie had turned away with the two children.

'Well, haven't we got a lot to tell Mummy and Daddy when we get back?' And haven't I got a lot that I don't want to share? Sherrie sighed to herself, glad of the distraction of Ben's hand in hers to stop her wayward thoughts.

I could so easily fall for him. Not much going for him, I don't think. Drop-dead gorgeous, efficient and caring in his work. And another strand I've seen today—he's a devoted father. But, even so, work comes first.

'Where's my daddy gone?' Amy's blue eyes gazed up appealingly.

'He had to look after a poorly man who had an accident. He'll fetch you very soon, but you can have some tea at our house with Ben.'

To Sherrie's relief, Ben was enough to distract Amy.

It's lucky I've got this evening with all the family to take my mind off him, she thought as, thankfully, she pushed open their front door and let herself, Ben and Amy into the hallway.

'Granma, Amy's come for tea.' Pulling Amy behind him, Ben raced to the kitchen.'

'Hello, Amy.' Sherrie's mother appeared in the doorway and raised an enquiring eyebrow at Sherrie.

'This is Amy, Mum, Dr O'Neill's daughter. There was a nasty accident at the fair and he asked if Amy could come with me for the time being while he went to the hospital with the patient.'

'You're all all right, are you?'

'Yes, we're fine, just longing for some tea.'

'Oh, this is Dr Wright, our locum.' Mrs Walker gestured to the young woman standing just inside the kitchen.

'How do you do?' With her fair hair pulled back in a clip and wearing large glasses, the visitor peered short-sightedly, before holding out her hand.

'Your father was about to show Linda the surgery when there was a call.'

'Poor old Dad,' Sherrie sighed. 'I'll just sort out the children and then show her, if you like.' But, chattering excitedly, they'd already disappeared so Sherrie led the way down the short passage to the extension, with Linda following close behind.

'It's very well fitted out, isn't it?' Linda stared around the consulting room, with its couch, desk and computer.

'Oh, Dad keeps himself pretty up to date, despite his old-fashioned ideas about running the practice. You must have made a terrific impression for him to allow you to take on his baby.'

'A touch of nepotism.' Linda laughed softly, the smile transforming her rather plain features. 'He was at medical school with my uncle.'

'Hope it's not going to be too much. Bit different from hospital, anyway.'

'I'm really looking forward to it.'

'Have you seen all you want? Dad should be home shortly and he can tell you what you want to know.'

Sherrie led the way back to the kitchen, but her mind was a tumult of speculation.

'Like some tea? I've just made a fresh pot.' Her mother smiled a welcome.

'Yes, please. Excuse, me, Linda. I'll just see what Ben and Amy are up to.'

They were having a rowdy game with Ben's toys. This was followed by a sticky tea, with Sherrie's mother enjoying every moment, then the two children curled up together on the settee to watch television.

A little while later Sherrie called, 'Amy, Daddy's here.' The little girl scampered into the hall at the sound of the doorbell and was whirled into Tim's arms.

'Been a good girl?'

'Certainly has.' Sherrie smiled at him across the top of Amy's head, surprised at the warmth that spread through her at the sight of his face.

'I'm sorry to have imposed on you. Now I must be very rude and dash. Where's your jacket, Amy?'

'Don't be silly. She's a delightful child, no trouble at all. Come and have a tea or coffee.'

Mrs Walker came to the door of the kitchen. 'Have you eaten? I could get you a sandwich or some cake.'

'I'm sorry, I really have to go.'

'Was he all right—the patient?' Sherrie buttoned Amy's jacket.

'Well, first of all, there was a possibility of amputation,' Tim said softly, 'and because I was more or less there when it happened, the family seemed to derive some comfort from my staying. But it's all under control now. They think they can save the leg after all. Then I had to collect my car. I'm sorry to have been so long.'

'That's no problem for us. My only concern was for Amy, but she's been fine. We'll be happy to have her visit at any time, won't we, Mum?'

'And we must return the compliment. Come on, miss, home now.' He lifted Amy and the sight of the chubby arms around his neck was curiously touching. He obviously adored his little daughter, but when duty called, well...

'Don't forget, ask Ben's mother if he can visit.'

Tim turned and waved as he reached the gate, accompanied by a vigorous wave from Amy.

CHAPTER THREE

FEELING decidedly jaded after her night out with her family, Sherrie hurried into the lift the following morning. Trying hard to smother a yawn, she barely noticed the only other occupant, who had his back to her, merely that he was wearing a yellow safety helmet.

'Good morning. Not speaking?' Tim's deep tones startled Sherrie. Hastily she tucked her paper under her arm and looked at him.

'Sorry. Good morning,' she babbled. 'I'm afraid I didn't recognize you there. Isn't it funny how often you only see what you expect to see? I saw the hard hat and nothing more registered. No wonder there are so many problems for the police with witnesses.'

'It's all right, you only had to say good morning.' He grinned as the lift clanked its slow way downwards. 'Has Ben recovered from the excitement of his trip to the fair? Amy couldn't stop talking about it for hours. It was Ben this and Ben that. Definitely a case of love at first sight.' He glanced slyly at her. 'Have you ever been afflicted in that way?'

'I don't know about love,' Sherrie said with a laugh. 'I was struck once. At a hospital fête. One of the doctors was selling balloons. You had to write your name and address and there was a prize for the balloon that travelled the furthest.' She smiled dreamily. 'I didn't get the prize for the furthest, just bought the greatest number of! I must have gone back about eight times!'

'Did he reciprocate?' Tim said softly.

'No, he fell for my best friend. What about you?' But at that moment the lift stopped and she and Tim walked along the corridor together. 'Ben and I had a great time yesterday. It was a pity there was that accident to spoil things at the end.'

'I called in at the ward this morning and he's doing very well. I must admit it's a relief that they were able to save the leg.'

Sherrie stopped beside the reception desk and picked up the numerous cards of waiting cases.

'Morning, Anna,' she murmured to the receptionist. 'Better get my skates on with this lot.'

'I should be able to put in a couple of hours this morning so, with any luck, we'll clear them quite quickly,' Tim interrupted.

Tim glanced over Sherrie's shoulder at the top card in her hand.

'And Sister is on triage, sorting out the serious from the trivial, so that will get things moving,' Anna added.

'Before I start, do you mind if I ask just one thing?' Sherrie looked up at Tim. 'Why on earth are you wearing that on your head?'

'I've been inspecting some of the new building work, and as I've no desire to become one of those statistics...' he pointed to the computer as it spewed out lists of names of patients, '...better safe than sorry.' He slipped the helmet off and ruffled his hair with his fingers.

Wish I could do that, Sherrie thought, her fingers aching with the desire to feel the thick texture of his hair. Hurriedly she turned towards the first of the patients on her list, horrified at the yearning she felt.

'Mr Rees?' She looked at the elderly man on the stretcher. His leg was at an awkward angle under the cover. She repeated his name more loudly as he looked at her blankly. 'It looks as though you've broken a bone in your hip.'

'Pardon?'

'Your hip.' Sherrie pointed to the injured area.

'Yes, I did slip and it's very painful.'

'Rest quietly. I'll get Nurse to give you a hand to get undressed.' Sherrie pulled up the safety bar at the side of the stretcher.

'How are you getting on?' Tim said some little while later as he went to yet another patient. 'All right?'

'Yes, I don't seem to be seeing the numbers of patients that I would like.' She looked at the cards in their slot on the desk and saw that Tim's contribution exceeded hers by about tenfold.

'Raring to go, eh? Don't be impatient,' Tim warned. 'Better to be a bit slow than to overlook something. I'm sure before long you'll be keeping up as well as anyone.'

'I'm not impatient, I just like to keep on top of things. Anyway, I must go and see to Mr Rees.'

'We'll have to do some more X-rays, I'm afraid. Mr Rees,' she said to her patient.

And so the morning wore on: sutures in a scalp wound, the toughness of the skin a shock as Sherrie pushed the needle through; a small boy who reminded her of Ben, crying as he had a severe abrasion on his leg bandaged; a broken nose that wouldn't stop bleeding, despite Sherrie's efforts, and splashed her white coat and dress; a middle-aged man rushed in from his office after a fainting attack and the tell-tale sweetness of acetone on his breath, betraying his diabetes even before the blood results came back from the laboratory.

Being kept so busy helped her to ignore any feelings she had towards Tim. Tim's attitude was, as always, completely professional, despite their shared day at the fair. She enjoyed the variety of cases, which helped to keep her on her toes, along with her desire to prove her ability in front of him.

'All right in here?' Tim's voice said quietly as he paused with a stretcher, the elderly woman's face covered by an oxygen mask. 'I'm just going to do another ECG and get a read-out. Nothing too significant on first glance, but a definite admission for Coronary Care.'

Walking swiftly to Reception, Sherrie picked up the next admission card.

'Is this the only one left, Anna?'

'Yes, apart from Mr Rees to go Orthopaedics. I reckon he's going to cause them fun and games. I don't think he's as hard of hearing as he makes out. Rob is taking him up there now.'

'Perhaps I'd better see him before he goes.'

'He's fine, I've checked him. Have a coffee,' Tim interrupted.

'Oh, the sweetest words I've heard this morning. I'm starving as well.'

'Well, if we ask nicely we might even be able to scrounge a sandwich from the nursing staff. This way.'

He walked to the area behind Reception and flung back the door to the rest room, which had only one other occupant. Sister glanced up briefly from her book.

'Morning, Sister. Coffee or tea, Sherrie?' He filled the kettle and plugged it in.

'Coffee for me, please. Black with sugar.'

With a grateful sigh Sherrie flopped into the chair by the window where there was a welcome breeze. 'I don't know how Casualty manages to get stuffy when the front doors are open nearly all the time.' Picking up a magazine, Sherrie fanned her face. 'That's wonderful.' She sniffed enthusiastically at the fragrant steam, rising from her cup, before taking a large swallow.

'And some cheese sandwiches. I suppose we can just help ourselves.'

'By all means.' Sister nodded. 'You can tell which sandwiches will go first, judging by whoever is on duty.'

'Cheese and pickle—great. In fact, it's a luxury I'd not expected, sandwiches as well as coffee.'

'It's so difficult to get a proper break for medical and nursing staff.'

'Isn't that true of the wards?' Sherrie took a large bite of bread.

'The workload doesn't fluctuate quite so vigorously as here. Plus the fact there's so little warning of what is coming through the door. Makes it more difficult to organise.'

'Sister.' Tim got to his feet as Sister went to the door. 'It is still all right to have that meeting this afternoon, isn't it?'

'Of course. We'll take a chance it might quieten down at about three o'clock, if that suits you.' She nodded and went swiftly from the room.

'I want to meet as many of the staff as I can,' Tim explained, 'lay out a few policies and, hopefully, get some feedback from the medical and nursing staff. If it's not too busy, of course.' He grinned lazily. 'What is your impression from a reasonably busy day? Not too tough?'

'Not at all. Anyway, I was spoilt in that you covered so many patients. I like the variety and the change of pace. There's a completely different feeling from the ward about the patients as they come in straight off the street and not in bed, undressed and at your mercy.'

'It puts paid to your killer instinct, does it? I agree, it is different, you have to accept them at their own valuation as an ordinary person rather than as an ailment. More coffee?'

'No thanks. But that was great.' She went to the sink and rinsed out her cup.

'No need to rush back yet. I reckon we've earned

ourselves a few minutes' grace. And I'm sure someone will call us if we're needed.'

Sherrie went back to her seat and picked up a
magazine. Her heart pounding like some adolescent
at being alone with Tim, she sighed.

'Penny for 'em.'

Sherrie gulped. 'Not interesting enough, even for a
penny.'

'Well, you could have fooled me, with that dreamy
expression.'

Her face coloured, and she flipped open the magazine. 'Let's have a look at my stars.'

'You don't believe in that, do you?'

'Not really, but there's no harm in the fun. I only
believe when it says something good. I don't believe
that millions of people all born on the same day are
alike, but an individual reading, with the astrologer
knowing time and place of birth, might be different.
Anyway, what is your star sign?'

'Scorpio. I think. I'm not sure. November the
tenth.'

'Yes, that's Scorpio. I see.'

'What's the matter? What horrible fate is in store
for me?'

'It's nothing like that. I was just thinking, Scorpios
are supposed to be very commanding and sexy.'

'Oh, really?'

Sherrie laughed out loud. 'You should see your
face. Every time anyone says they don't believe in the
stars you only have to say their sign is passionate or
sexy and immediately they preen and want to know
more.' I don't need to know his star sign to know he

is sexy, Sherrie thought. With that sensual mouth, he couldn't be anything else.

'You've got a lovely laugh.' Tim smiled. 'Of course I'm interested in being told I should be sexy. It's only natural, isn't it?'

'I'm afraid you're going to be a bit disappointed with today's forecast. Not very interesting.' Sherrie folded back the page. '"Today will see the start of a new venture that can lead to great things. Someone new in your life could become important."'

'Sorry, I still think it's rubbish. What is your forecast for the day?'

'Let's see. Aries.'

'What are they supposed to be like?'

'Very bossy and dramatic, don't suffer fools gladly and very loyal friends.'

'I can imagine you being bossy.'

'Never. Anyway, "Today will mark the start of a new relationship which could become important."'

'That's almost exactly the same as mine.'

'Perhaps our lives are taking a similar direction. But, then you don't have to worry as you don't believe in them.' She shrugged and put the magazine on the table.

The door flew back. 'There's been a road accident, driver plus three passengers. I've not assessed the injuries completely so far.' Pushing up her sleeves, ready for action, Sister hurried towards the main area.

It was a very different place from earlier, seeming to be full of trolleys, with paramedics and nurses milling around.

'Which had I better see first, Sister?'

'That man there, I think. Front-seat passenger. Crushed chest and lost a lot of blood.'

Sherrie studied the man Sister had indicated. Blood was already seeping through the blanket covering him. His head was held steady on the stretcher by a broad band of Elastoplast across his forehead and his eyes were closed, seemingly unaware of the controlled chaos around him. With Rob following close behind, pushing a trolley, Sherrie went to the cubicle to begin her examination.

'Fractured ribs, possibly blood in the chest cavity.' Carefully Sherrie listened to the man's chest. 'We'll need a chest drain after X-rays. I can't hear any breath sounds on the right at all, Rob.'

'I'll get X-ray here and a trolley for putting in a drain.'

'Who's next?'

'The man in the wheelchair. It looks as though he's got away with no more than a broken ankle.' Sister came up behind her. 'I've asked for portable X-rays on your patient so they may as well do the others as well.'

In a surprisingly short time the general flurry cleared and, much sooner than Sherrie would have expected, the patients had been transferred to their respective wards. Sherrie slumped in a chair in the reception area, glad to seize a few minutes' respite before Tim's meeting.

'Now we've got to listen to our leader,' Sherrie grumbled to her friend, Liz, house officer in medicine, as they sat in the front row of chairs in the main casualty area, waiting for Tim and other staff to arrive. Before long there was a general buzz of conversation and Sherrie was surprised at the numbers that had turned up.

'The only trouble with any group of doctors are the bleepers. Won't be long now before they start interrupting things. Wonder what the collective noun is for a group of doctors?'

'I think it should be a bleep of doctors,' Liz said with a giggle as the first one sounded just as Tim arrived and stood at the front. Unusually formal in a tailored suit and pale blue shirt with matching tie, he put his white coat beside him on a chair.

'Thank you all for coming here this afternoon. I know any spare time is usually spent in more worthwhile pursuits, like catching up on one's sleep.' His eyes seemed to bore directly into Sherrie's.

'On each of your seats there is a brief written summary of what I'm hoping to do, which you can study later. It consists of an emergency call-out service so that we have a roster of volunteer medical staff available on call to go out to more serious cases with the ambulance.

'As I'm sure you all know, the first hour is the "golden hour" and if we can get more extensive treatment to the patient during that time it should improve the chances of recovery, not only for accidents but also for heart attacks and stroke victims as well.' He shuffled the papers on his desk. 'It will necessitate a more fully equipped ambulance which will be based here, rather than at the ambulance station.'

Removing his glasses, he looked around at everyone. 'Any questions so far?'

In the front row, Sherrie raised her hand. Gosh, she thought, like going back to school.

'Has the ambulance service been consulted on this, and would the ambulance be available for other hospitals in the area? In which case, would they provide their own medical staff? And also, what more—?'

'As the paramedics are trained to intubate, put up infusions and monitor heart rhythms, what do they feel about this idea?' interrupted a voice from the back.

'And would the shifts be an extra to our normal working week? If not, how would it affect proper medical cover in the specialties?' a third person asked.

'Give the guy a break,' Liz murmured under her breath.

'Whoa, please, everyone. I'm still working on basics and, with your questions here today, I realise there'll have to be a lot more research. It will take time to organise and there will be teething problems, but I saw a similar scheme in the United States and they claimed it had reduced the mortality on urgent admissions by twenty per cent.' Tim raised his hand.

'I know statistics can be used to prove anything, but I do think it will be worth study in more detail and further discussion.'

Sherrie wouldn't have thought it possible, but she felt almost sorry for Tim as he collected his paperwork together. 'Well, at least I've given you all something to think about and I'll welcome any suggestions anyone may come up with. We should be aware that many smaller casualty departments are being closed and any extra service we can offer will stand us in good stead.

'Once again, thank you all for taking the time to come here today.'

The group gradually dissipated, the buzz of voices as they left the department audible even when most had left the room.

'Will you volunteer?' Liz turned her dark eyes in Sherrie's direction as they walked towards Reception.

'Probably. I think I would enjoy it and it must be good experience. Anna...' she turned to the girl behind the desk '...I have to go to the library to pick up some books. I'll only be gone a few minutes and I've got my bleeper so call me and I'll come running to the rescue.'

'I'll walk down with you.' Liz stepped out alongside. 'I hadn't thought of that before. It must be difficult to get away from A and E even when it's quiet.'

'Well, I think Tim is around, anyway, so who needs me?'

'He does a lot of hands-on work, doesn't he? More than most consultants.' Liz giggled as they walked along the drive. 'I wouldn't mind his hands on me, to tell you the truth.'

'Oh, Liz you're incorrigible.' Sherrie stifled a laugh.

'Come on, don't act all sweet and innocent with me. Even though you've sworn yourself to your profession—'

'I've not done any such thing.'

'Well, close. You don't *have* to remain celibate.

Even you, with your dislike of getting involved with another member of staff, must admit that it could be pretty difficult to avoid it here. Is he married?'

'Liz, you're the end. I don't know.' Sherrie grinned mischievously. 'Perhaps you could find out for me?' She paused. 'Actually, he has a partner and a little girl.'

Liz looked back at her, her dark eyes wide. 'How did you find that out? You *are* interested in our Doctor Tim.'

'Shh, not so loud.' But it was too late. Footsteps on the gravel drive behind them caught up and Tim's deep voice spoke from over Sherrie's shoulder.

'Sorry. Didn't mean to eavesdrop. Interested in what?'

'Nothing,' Sherrie said abruptly, and turned onto the path leading to the library. 'Ciao, Liz, see you later.'

She hoped her wave was more nonchalant than the expression on her face. Despite her brave words to Liz, she *was* interested, she had to admit.

Every time she went into a cubicle in Casualty she had her fingers crossed that he might be there. The sound of his voice or an unexpected meeting made her pulses race, and the day at the fair was set like a jewel in her memory just because she'd been with Tim. God forbid he should find out—she'd die. She wasn't interested in involvement with any other member of staff, but there was something about him... Quickly, she pressed the coding for the library entry.

'Allow me.' An arm reached across her shoulder and pushed back the door.

'Are you following me?'

'Of course not.' Tim smiled. 'It's just that I haven't the code number for this door so you being here is very convenient.' He stepped past her and held the door ajar, before scribbling details on the card the librarian gave him then disappearing into the aisle of reference books. As he walked away he murmured quietly, 'See you anon, no doubt. I hope you can hold the fort for the remainder of the day.'

'Of course. Just think of the excellent teacher I have.' She quickly found the book on neurology she wanted and tucked it under her arm. 'Oh, well, back to the paperwork, I suppose.' Disappointed that Tim didn't glance up as she left, she hurried back to A and E.

CHAPTER FOUR

'HEY, Sherrie, look at this!' One of the group gathered round the on-call listing called to her as she walked into the commonroom.

'You're one of the first to do this new casualty duty—with Tim O'Neill, starting tonight,' Liz said enviously.

'Oh, no.' Sherrie grimaced. 'I had no idea we would be starting it so soon. I can think of plenty of other things I'd rather be doing.' Rather than working closely with Tim? her inner self asked. She tossed her head and curled up in a deep armchair, its dark blue material flattering her fair skin and copper hair.

'Such as?' Liz protested. 'It's only one night in two weeks. And you must have put your name down.' She leant over the chair. 'Scared to be spending time with him alone?' she muttered.

'Don't be daft. I see our new consultant at work every day, without having to spend an evening in his company. I was going with David to see that co-median, Bob Miller.'

'I'll cover your shift for you if you like,' Liz said eagerly.

'Actually, Tim won't agree to last-minute changes. I still think the paramedics aren't going to be too impressed at us turning up at the scene of accidents and taking over.'

'Don't forget, the first hour after the accident is the "golden hour" and to have medical help immediately available can make quite a difference to the outcome of patients' recovery. Not only accidents, but heart attacks, and so on,' Liz said facetiously.

'I know, I know, it's a good idea, really. But with a bit of luck I might not be called out. Let's see what's on the box just in case.'

'I'm not sure how the system works exactly.' Kumar, who worked on the surgical unit, flopped down near Sherrie and stretched out his long legs in front of him.

'The idea is to have a series of volunteers—volunteers, mind you—to be on call in case of serious accidents, a bit like the maternity flying squad, to go to the scene and liaise with the emergency services.'

'Like a major alert, then.'

'Not exactly. It's going to be used not only for motorway accidents but in other cases as well. And there is talk of eventually sharing a helicopter with the police for taking patients to more distant specialised units.'

'I must say, our new consultant seems very dynamic.'

'I don't wish to sound critical,' Sherrie said with a giggle, 'but God knows where we'd land a helicopter in this hospital. Trying to park my Mini is enough of a nightmare.'

'Behind A and E, I think. They're clearing ground for it at the same time as building the extension.'

'More lovely beech trees gone,' sighed Sherrie.

'Damn, there's my bleeper.' Liz stared at the digital

display. 'Not Mallory Ward again. I bet Mrs Tomkins's drip has packed up. See you.' She hurried from the room and soon all the other occupants disappeared, leaving Sherrie thumbing disconsolately through the TV guide. Nothing among the old films attracted her interest so she pulled out her notebook and read through the details of the patients of the day.

'It doesn't seem possible that we dealt with so many cases.' She whistled softly under her breath. 'Even though a lot were relatively minor injuries.' She sighed.

She wasn't so sure now that she was going to be able to cope with this job. Each day in Tim's company increased her liking for him and her feelings weren't altered by his always totally professional approach. Perhaps it wasn't anything to do with that, but something wasn't quite right with how she felt.

In fact, the shifts on Casualty were kinder than on many wards, with at least one night in three off completely. The prospect of working in the accident department had seemed so exciting and she'd been thrilled when she'd been accepted for the post, but some of her original enthusiasm seemed to be fading.

'Wonder what would happen if you refused to do one of the shifts,' she muttered aloud. 'Wonder if medical staff have ever gone on strike. A very tempting thought sometimes. Trouble is, management and senior personnel know they have us over a barrel because we would never consider it in case it harmed the patients.'

'Talking to yourself? You know what that's the first sign of, don't you?'

Embarrassed, Sherrie glanced over the back of the chair. 'Do you mean madness? No, you've got that wrong. The first sign of insanity, at least in my schooldays, was to have hair growing on the palms of your hands. And the second...' she grinned mischievously '...was to look at them.'

Grinning with her, Tim stopped studying his hands and quickly thrust them into the pockets of his white coat. 'You caught me there. All set for this evening? You're not proposing to wear that lovely outfit, are you?' Tim gazed at her assessingly.

'I was all dressed to go out, just in case, and I thought I would just put my white coat over it if we are called. But perhaps I'd better change into theatre top and trousers.'

'Are you all right? You seem a bit down.'

'I would far rather have been on my way to my date, instead of sitting here waiting for the phone to ring.'

'And I would far rather have been on my way home to Amy,' Tim countered.

'How is she?'

'She's fine, but has been a bit out of hand the last few days.'

'I bet that's Ben's influence.' Sherrie laughed. 'I'm surprised she's at all controllable after an afternoon in his company.'

'Don't malign your nephew. He may be naughty but, with his auntie's charm, he should be able to sail through life.' Tim pulled forward an upright chair and straddled it, his arms leaning on the back, while he studied her intently with those piercing eyes. Now that they were closer Sherrie thought the colour was more a deep grey-blue. 'Tell me, are you engaged or spoken for?'

Sherrie slowly shook her head. 'You asked me that before. I'm too career-minded at present. No wedding bells or hearts and flowers for me.'

'Not at all? Why is that? A broken heart in the past? Whatever the reason, it's good to know we'll have your undivided attention.'

'I didn't say that. I'd be pretty boring if all I thought about was work.' Made uncomfortable by his intense stare, she fidgeted and looked away.

'I can't imagine you ever being boring. While we've got some quiet time together, tell me something about yourself. As I didn't get to do the interviews I missed out on a lot of background information about the team.'

'What can I tell you? You can see from my CV where I've worked before, such as it is.'

'Not that sort of thing. What made you come into medicine, for a start?'

'My father is a doctor and I always enjoyed all the stories he told us when we were kids about hospital life. And it's true what he said once—all that extra knowledge is like being a member of a very exclusive club. Though magazines have so many articles these days, Joe Public is probably better informed than we are.'

'That's true. And doctors are certainly not considered to be gods any more.'

'Would you want them to be? I think it's far more

healthy that patients question things, rather than take everything as gospel.'

'As long as it doesn't get to suing all the time, as has happened in the States. That can cloud your medical judgement if you're not careful.'

'I can't imagine you ever being swayed in that way.' She straightened in her chair.

'Hopefully not. Enough of medical matters. What are your interests outside work?'

'Music of all sorts, going to discos, old-fashioned films—the ones that make you cry—yoga to keep me calm and lots of walking. Oh, and cooking. Like my mother, I'm a very good cook.'

'What do you like to cook? We'd make a good team, then. I'm a very good eater.'

Sherrie studied the frame of the man in front of her—wide shoulders, trim waist and long, denim-clad legs.

'Not to excess, though, by the look of you. I'm used to the male of the species being good trencher-men because of my brothers. My poor mother, I don't know how she stands it. The food looks enough to feed an army, and she barely has time to set it on the table before the locusts swoop and it's gone. I thought that once they'd passed their teens it might get better, but I think she'll miss it when they *all* leave home.'

'Something intrigues me. Where did you get such an unusual name? Is there Spanish blood in your family? If there is it's certainly not been passed on to you, though your eyes are sherry-coloured.'

'I have three older brothers and when my parents

realised that they'd got their longed-for girl at last they named me after Jerez in Spain.'

'Run that by me again. Why after a place?'

Sherrie could feel the warmth tinging her cheeks. 'Because that's where I was conceived,' she murmured. I can't believe I'm actually shy at saying such a thing, she chided herself. Hopefully the dim light of the commonroom was enough to hide her blushes.

'Are you blushing, Dr Walker? We all have to be conceived somewhere. It's nothing to be shy about.'

He knows I'm embarrassed. How stupid, for a doctor of all people.

'If you'll excuse me, I'd better go and change into something more workmanlike.'

'It's a pity you have to do that, you look so delightful, but it makes sense not to risk spoiling your clothes. Oh, here we go.' Tim looked at his bleeper as it sounded, then hurried to the phone. 'How many? One, really serious, as far as you can tell. Don't need me to tell you not to move him. Oh, you can't anyway.'

Quickly Sherrie dashed to the cloakroom, slipped on the loose theatre top and trousers and flung her white coat over her shoulders.

'Come on. Not far to go.' Tim opened the main door when she returned and ushered Sherrie through.

'What's happened?' she muttered breathlessly as she tried to keep up in her strappy sandals. They were all right for an evening out, but not now as they hurried towards Casualty. Tim's long-legged stride easily covered the ground. 'Do we need the full works and all the equipment?' she puffed.

'Yes, but not far to carry it. One of the earth-movers on the casualty site toppled over and the driver is trapped underneath.'

'Oh, no! That sounds grim. How on earth are we going to deal with that?'

'The fire service has been notified, and the anaes-thetist on call has checked that there is a bed available in Intensive Care.'

'Someone must have been talking very quickly if they managed to get that much information to you in the time you were on the phone.'

Suddenly Sherrie tripped and she couldn't prevent a small cry of distress as her ankle twisted painfully under her. Biting her lip, she limped behind Tim.

'What are you doing?' he said sharply.

'I've twisted my ankle. You go on.'

'It's only a few paces. I'll carry you.'

'Don't be silly.' He ignored her embarrassed pro-test and swung her into his arms.

Acutely aware of the warmth of his skin through the cotton shirt and the closeness of his face, which smelt faintly of fresh aftershave, she stared in all di-rections, trying not to meet his eyes, desperate to reach Casualty.

He backed through the swing door with her still in his arms.

'Very Clark Gable in *Gone with the Wind*,' Sherrie muttered, almost overcome with embarrassment.

'Let me have a look.' With scant ceremony, Tim lowered Sherrie into the nearest chair and took her foot on his lap. 'No sign of a fracture,' he murmured gently, rotating her ankle.

'Kate,' he called to the nearby nurse, 'can you put an Elastoplast support bandage on Sherrie's ankle, please?' He turned to Sherrie. 'Will you be all right? I need you out there immediately.'

Wow, she thought, sorry about your foot, Sherrie, hope it's not too painful, Sherrie. Talk about TLC. Perhaps she was being unfair. Hurting her ankle couldn't have come at a worse time. Casualty for once was eerily silent, all the staff except a receptionist and one senior nurse missing, and there seemed to be only one patient, waiting in a cubicle.

Trying hard to disguise her limp, Sherrie hurried through to the rear of the building and paused, horrified at the sight that confronted them. The huge yellow machine, like some prehistoric monster, lay on its side, one large wheel slowly revolving. Its driver was barely visible, just a helmeted head in the ditch.

'The fire service will bring some lamps, I expect. In the meantime, we've got arc lamps we used when we were working earlier in the year.' Bill, the site manager, a stockily built man in his fifties, hurried forward to greet them, a worried frown corrugating his pleasant face.

'I've no idea how this happened. We were about to pack up, and Stan was lining up the machine for the morning. Suddenly he let out this great yell and the bloody thing tilted slowly onto its side. I think the edge of the trench must have been crumbly from all the rain we've had.'

'Have all your men gone home?' Tim led the way and crouched, looking down at the injured man.

'We've still got one or two on site.'

'Look at him.' Tim nudged Sherrie. 'Chest injuries for sure. The arm of the machine is lying right across him. Hopefully, his helmet has saved him from any damage to his head. I'm going to go down into the ditch and try and assess him.'

'I'm not too sure about that, Doc. I'd rather wait till the fire service gets here to prop up the machine.'

'Doc.' Very informal. Sherrie raised surprised eyebrows.

Tim turned to face Bill. 'We might not be able to wait. We might have to find some way to lever it ourselves.'

'I'll get all the gear,' said Sherrie anxiously, hovering to one side.

'Right. Oxygen, of course, stuff in case we can manage an arterial line. We'll need a base line gas done. I'd like to avoid a chest drain unless we absolutely have to. I'd rather wait for that until after a chest X-ray, anyway.'

Hastily Sherrie raced back through the doors of Casualty, her sprained ankle forgotten, and grabbed a trolley. It took only moments to load it, then she pushed it back to the site of the accident, rattling over the uneven ground. To her relief, as she set the trolley near to the machine a two-tone alarm could be heard and a fire engine raced into view.

'I knew we should never have had this extension built. It's judgement for destroying all those lovely beech trees and churning up the grass banks.'

'Don't be stupid. That's got nothing to do with the accident.' Tim glared as he heard her words. His face was lit by the backdrop of overhead light, casting deep shadows under the eyes and making him appear almost satanic.

'I didn't mean any personal criticism. I know this extension is your pride and joy.'

But Tim wasn't listening. The next half-hour was a manic scramble, with more medical and nursing staff appearing and the firemen setting up their equipment—cutting gear, air bags and a large lifting lever.

'What are you doing?' the senior officer said sharply as Tim went to the end of the trench and leapt in lightly beside the injured man. 'We don't want to have two of you to rescue.'

'I won't be a moment, I promise. Just a quick assessment and then we'll be able to see the best way to get him out.'

'Don't know about the best way.' The fire officer leapt in beside Tim. 'There may be only one way. We'll have to support this before we can do anything.'

'He's got the arm of the machine right across his chest and that will have to be moved very carefully. You might not be able to use cutting equipment if we're giving him oxygen.'

'You do your job, I'll do mine and we'll try not to clash.'

Sherrie realised she was holding her breath as Tim gradually slid his stethoscope under the edge of Stan's overalls. Even from where she was standing, she could see Stan's lips were the colour of Parma violets. His breathing was clearly audible.

At least he was still alive. Trying to anticipate what was wanted, she took the small oxygen cylinder from the trolley and connected it to the face mask. A terrible noise like the growl of some large beast made her spin on her heel.

'Right, Doctor, out now. And I mean *now*.' The fire officer's shout startled them all.

The machine rocked slightly as Tim and the fire officer scrambled over the edge of the trench.

'He must be in a lot of pain and he desperately needs oxygen. We can't just leave him like that. Can you shore up the machine enough for me to get down there and do that? No heroics, I promise.' Tim took the hard hat passed to him by Bill.

'Let's see what we can do.'

'Right.' Tim turned to Sherrie. 'Draw me up some morphine, please, and I'll have the small oxygen cylinder. Might be a good idea to give Stan some Valium as well.'

'Won't that depress his breathing even more?' Sherrie queried as she assembled the syringes and doses of drugs.

'We'll have to chance that. Apparently, in severe accidents the advantages of Valium or its equivalent outweigh the problems.'

'What happens now?' Sherrie stared anxiously at the fire officer.

'What happens now is that we try and get that beggar wedged enough to hold it while we bring him out. If you wouldn't mind getting out of the way, miss.'

'I'm not miss, I'm a doctor.'

'Not a pretty little thing like you.' His eyes twinkled mischievously as he pushed back his helmet.

'That is the end,' Sherrie complained.

'Sorry, *doctor*, if you could get out of the way and

take your paraphernalia right over there, if possible, unless the doctor needs anything else, of course. Well clear of the field of operations, you might say.'

Barely had Sherrie pushed the trolley to one side when there was a call from Tim. 'I think I'll have to inject into his jugular vein. I can't reach any of the smaller ones, but you might be able to. Can you possibly come down? With you being much smaller, you might be able to get to his wrist more easily than I can,' Tim said softly.

Sherrie slithered down the muddy red surface.

'I've still got the morphine,' said Tim, 'but I think I'll forget the Valium for the moment. I think you're right on that. Try and reach his chest. I'm praying he hasn't fractured his sternum or we'll have big trouble.'

'What could be worse than it is now?' Taking the syringe from the receiver, Sherrie wriggled on her stomach and managed to take hold of an arm. There was a heart-rending groan. 'All right, Stan, I'm going to give you something for the pain.' It felt as though his arm was broken but, gently squeezing his wrist, she brought a vein into view and injected the painkiller.

'I've also given up on the idea of an arterial stab. Just put on the pulse oximeter and we'll leave it at that.'

'What was that noise?' Fearfully Sherrie looked up at the creaking sound from above and to her horror saw a slight rocking action from the machine.

'Oy, time to get out of there.' The helmeted face of the senior fire officer peered down at them. 'Lift the doctor up to me and I'll pull her clear. Can you manage this slope, Doctor?'

Her heart beating fearfully, Sherrie raised her arms and felt the strength of Tim's hands at her waist. With no sign of effort, he held her aloft and two firemen each seized a hand and pulled her over the edge of the trench.

'Oh, God, look at me,' she wailed. Her front was smothered in red mud and the toes of her sandals were half on and half off from wriggling on her stomach.

Relief at getting out of danger brought on a surge of adrenalin, and Sherrie surprised herself by playfully punching Tim on the arm.

'Let's get back to business. Now that we've finished with the heroics I want you two out of the way,' said the fire officer.

'Hadn't we better stay close at hand in case?' Sherrie swallowed nervously.

'You do as you're told,' Tim said sternly. 'I'm not having you in the way.'

'I won't be in the way,' she muttered rebelliously, but with poor grace she moved back slightly. Didn't Tim trust her or something?

'How much will he feel when we start moving him?' The fire officer pointed into the trench with his thumb.

'Hopefully, not too much, but we didn't give a very large dose of painkiller because it might be easier if Stan's able to understand a bit of what you're saying.'

'Right, you stand well back,' Tim said sharply to Sherrie. Sherrie stood away from the trench and wrapped her white coat around her, suddenly cold, and watched in admiration as the emergency team somehow managed to lever the J.C.B. enough to get in a small metal scoop stretcher.

'Is the lady doctor still there?' A voice echoed up from the depths.

Quickly Sherrie peered over. 'Yes, is there any problem?'

'We need someone small to get close and sort out these straps. Could you bear to come down again?'

'Of course.'

'Just a minute, put this on.' Bill reached behind her and handed her a yellow work helmet.

'Boy, do you look cute.' Tim grinned.

'I'm twenty-seven years old, for goodness' sake, and a qualified doctor,' Sherrie muttered through clenched teeth. 'I'm not cute.'

'You are, though. Only do what is essential. I want you out of there as soon as possible.' Handing her stethoscope to Tim, she slithered down the slope towards the two paramedics and the fire officer.

'Sorry to ask you to do this, but I think your smaller frame might be able to get closer.'

Swiftly Sherrie glanced at the pulse oximeter clipped to Stan's finger and saw that his blood oxygen levels had fallen, despite the face mask.

'We'll have to get a move on,' she whispered. 'The levels of oxygen in his blood are getting low.'

'I noticed that,' the paramedic muttered.

'Right, one final push.'

'Hang on, I'll give him a bit more morphine.' Swiftly she took the syringe and injected their now-unconscious patient. 'Where are these straps?'

'We've fixed the chest ones. There's one to go round the top of his thighs.'

'Commando time again.' Digging her elbows into the soft earth, Sherrie stretched across and fastened the straps. 'That's it.'

'Great. Thanks, Doctor. You get on back. Can you make it up the slope?'

Sherrie needed no encouragement. She glanced warily in the direction of the ominous creakings above her head.

'Here you are.' She looked up to see Tim, leaning over the edge, and he took her hands and pulled her to the rim.

'Oh, come on. Get a move on.' She hopped anxiously from one foot to the other, not wanting to get in the way but at the same time not wanting to move too far in case she was needed.

'Come here. What a heroine.' Pulling her to him, Tim's arms enfolded her in a mighty hug.

'What about all this mud?'

'Well, I'm not exactly the picture of sartorial elegance myself. I don't mind a bit of mud.'

Gratefully, Sherrie gave herself up to the warmth of his body and the comfort of his arms. He looked down at her. 'You're right—not so ethereal, are you? But it was a bit stupid to go down again.'

'I could hardly not do it, even though I was scared to death down there—weren't you? I don't know how they all deal with life-threatening emergencies under those conditions.'

Savouring Tim's closeness and the feel of him, she

didn't notice the heads appear over the rim until a small cheer broke out from the other site workers.

'Right, let's get him inside.' Placing the injured man carefully on the stretcher, the entourage hurried into the main casualty area, where in moments a team descended on them.

'This is what I want.' Tim clapped his hands to get their attention. 'Chest X-ray, arterial line and a base line gas done, set-up for chest drain, a couple of units of type O blood. In the meantime, cross-match four units of blood, and let ITU know we'll be with them shortly. Don't take too long.'

'Yes, sir. We do know all that.' Sherrie saluted, then put a needle into the patient's artery at the wrist and took a specimen of blood. 'I think Tim's got consultantitis.'

'What?' Kate grinned as she helped to cut off Stan's overalls.

'Consultantitis, consultant—get it? I'll just get this blood gas done. Looks pretty blue.' Sherrie held the syringe up to the light and examined it carefully, then gasped at the sound of a grumbling crash from outside. 'What was that?' she asked, wide-eyed, as two nurses scurried round.

'You got him out just in time,' muttered one. 'That was the earth-mover, just fallen completely into the trench.'

'Oh, my God. Was everybody clear?' For a moment Sherrie couldn't move, her legs feeling like jelly as she realised the implications. Taking a deep breath, she gave a hand as the nurses removed Stan's overalls and wrapped him in a foil warming blanket. One nurse fitted a neck support, another set up a trolley with the necessary equipment and a third washed off the mud from Stan's chest ready to attach the electrodes for the ECG.

Everything going well, thought Sherrie.

'What's his blood pressure?'

'Ninety over forty.'

'Surprisingly good under the circumstances. We're just about ready to take him upstairs.' Tim nodded across the heads. 'Two fractured ribs but not his sternum, thank God, though I'll get onto the chest people to have a look.' The stretcher and ventilator were a tight fit in the lift, with an anaesthetist, Tim and two nurses.

'I'll come up the stairs,' Sherrie said hastily and set off at a trot. Her legs were shaking and her ankle throbbed as she puffed up the last turn, arriving at the same time as the lift. When she looked at her watch she was amazed to see they'd been over two hours outside. Through the corridor window the evening was drawing in, darkening the sky.

The door to the intensive care unit was open and a staff nurse was waiting for their arrival.

'Here you are, bed one,' she instructed, pointing to the first cubicle, and the team lifted Stan into bed.

One nurse attached electrodes to give a reading of the heart and another connected the ventilator to the tube in Stan's mouth. His breathing settled to a more normal rate and infusions were restarted.

'Have you been given a history?' Sherrie asked the registrar on call.

'Only briefly. I heard how it happened, followed by

lots of heroics from the medical staff, I gather.' He busied himself as Sherrie gave the report.

'Crushed chest, two fractured ribs on the right. We've put in a chest drain, as you can see, and the bleeding seems to be easing off. Fractured radius on the right as well, possibly when he put up his arm to try and protect himself. Blood gases pretty poor, though they've improved in the last half-hour. He will also need warming up—temperature only 34°C.'

'Thanks. Has anyone contacted the family?'

'Not to my knowledge. I was off to get the site foreman to contact them now so I can talk to them. Is there anything else you want from us?'

'I don't think so. I'll give you a call if I need you.'

'Right. Good luck.'

She went into Stan's cubicle on the way out. Gently, Sherrie squeezed his hand. He lay peacefully on his back, his colour almost normal. 'All right, now, Stan, that's the worst over. They'll take good care of you here.'

Picking up her stethoscope, Sherrie set off down the stairs. Her legs were trembling and her back aching by the time she reached the accident department.

'Is Tim with you?' Staff Nurse looked up as Sherrie reached the reception desk.

'No, he's still helping to sort out everything on ITU.' Sherrie grinned mischievously. 'Bet they love that.'

'He is a bit new-broomish, isn't he? But very good for all that,' Staff acknowledged.

'There's nothing else that I should be dealing with

here, is there?' asked Sherrie. 'If not, I'm going to collapse in a chair with a large hot mug of coffee.'

'Sit there for a moment, and I'll put the kettle on.'

Sherrie sank back with a grateful sigh and minutes later tackled coffee and biscuits, nodding as Tim came through the door.

'Well, that wasn't too bad, was it?' he said as he stretched out in the chair opposite, both hands curled around his coffee-mug.

'Well, it certainly wasn't boring. I don't know about not too bad.' Sherrie's eyes widened as she remembered the scramble in the ditch and the difficulty of getting to the patient, with ominous noises over their heads as they worked.

'I think the fire officers deserve a medal, putting their lives in danger every day. Must be hell for their nearest and dearest.'

'I don't think we were in too much danger—the machine was pretty firmly wedged. Well, until that last part.'

'Come in,' she called to the tap at the door and Bill's amiable face appeared.

'They asked me upstairs about getting in touch with Stan's family and I've brought his address and telephone number. How badly is he hurt? I wonder if I'd better have a word with his wife first and give her some warning.'

'Perhaps that would be better, especially if you know her.' Tim passed the telephone across the room. 'Would you like a coffee?'

'Very milky and sweet, please.' Bill pressed a sequence of numbers before launching into his explanation, going on to reassure, 'No, it's not as bad as it sounds, Janet. He's in Intensive Care and the doctor is waiting to have a word.'

Sherrie stretched out her hand but wasn't surprised when Bill automatically passed the receiver to Tim.

Still, she had to admit, his voice was wonderfully soothing and his explanation clear and concise.

'No, you're very welcome to come and see him. He is all connected to tubes and lines and he can't speak because of the tube in his mouth. Have you got someone to bring you in? Good, I'll still be here and will be able to explain everything more fully.'

He rang off and turned to Sherrie. 'I think we'd better stay here. If any further calls come in we can be on the spot. You were great tonight. I don't expect you to deal with the cases coming through the door, of course.'

'Well, thanks a lot. It must be the tension, but I'm shattered. I don't think I could sleep if I tried. I'm not sure if it's worth going to bed and taking a chance on being woken up or whether to wait and see what happens.' She smothered a yawn. 'I must try to be brighter than this before my night off.'

'Heavy date, eh?' Tim raised his eyebrows at her.

'Nothing so exciting, though that's hardly fair. A hen-night—one of the staff nurses is getting married soon.'

'Well, I'm on my way. Enjoy yourself if I don't see you again before then. I'm going to try and sort out some notes for a lecture. If I'm up and about I may as well make use of the time.'

'Don't you ever get tired? I'll say goodnight, then,

Superman.' Sherrie grinned as she set off along the corridor towards the doctors' quarters, and the on-call bedroom. 'I'll keep my fingers crossed that we *don't* see each other again tonight, if you see what I mean.'

She limped away, very doubtful that she would be able to sleep. It wasn't only the adrenalin from dealing with Stan's accident, but also her growing feelings for Tim, which kept bubbling to the surface, and she knew that it would be difficult, if not impossible, to smother those.

CHAPTER FIVE

'Come in!' Sherrie turned from a final look in the dressing-table mirror, glancing at—but not really seeing—the plainly furnished and functional room.

'Are you ready?' Liz stood in the doorway.

'As ready as I'll ever be. God, look at those shadows under my eyes. And that's with my full warpaint on.' Sherrie smoothed the gold-flecked top snugly over her skirt and pulled on her shoes. 'I've a horrible feeling that Kelly's hen night is not going to be my cup of tea.'

'Don't be such an old misery. You'll enjoy it when you get there, you know you will. What do you think of my new top?' Liz held her arms in the air and twirled in the doorway.

'Great, Liz, really suits you.' Sherrie picked up her bag, checked the contents, then joined Liz, slamming and locking the bedroom door behind her as she left.

'I really think it's about time I started looking for my own place. Living in a place like a boarding school at my age is ridiculous and it's time I moved all my stuff from my parents.'

'But,' Liz objected, 'it's so convenient, especially when you're on call.'

'Hey, Sherrie, Liz, over here.' The voices of the rest of the party echoed in the foyer and it wasn't long before eight laughing women climbed into the taxis waiting outside.

Sounding like excited teenagers, with everyone talking at once, it was a few moments before Sherrie was able to find out the plans for the evening. 'Where are we going?'

'The wine bar first for a drink, then to that new Greek restaurant, the Olive Grove.'

'I don't really like Greek food,' protested Anna, one of the group.

'Never mind, it's served by a load of gorgeous Greek hunks so you won't have to worry about the food.'

'Kelly, you're not supposed to have thoughts like that. Two more days and then it's undying love to one man.'

'All the more reason to let my hair down tonight.' Kelly grinned saucily.

The bar was full and the noisy hum of voices and clink of glasses made conversation impossible so it wasn't long before they decided to move on to the restaurant.

'Let's walk, it won't take us long.'

'That's good, I'm starving,' Sherrie groaned. 'I've been saving myself and, unlike Anna, I love Greek food. Whether it will taste quite the same when you're not in some little taverna under brilliant Mediterranean skies I don't know.'

They walked quickly through the cold night air, a capricious wind stirring the leaves in the gutter and rattling an overhead shop sign.

'I hate the winter,' Kelly sighed.

'It's not winter, it's early spring. Never mind. Lovely West Indies in a couple of days, you lucky so-and-so.' Liz laughed. 'All the sun you could want.'

They hurried through the door of the restaurant. A waiter, dressed in tight-fitting black trousers and a crisp white shirt, greeted them. 'May I take your coats, please, ladies, and would you like a drink?'

'We'll have some white wine at the table. Is that all right for everyone?' Kelly followed the waiter to a table set back from the small dance floor.

'This is nice.' Sherrie glanced around at the embroidered white cloths and candles on each table. Busts of Greek gods sat in small alcoves around the walls. Laughing, they crammed into their seats.

'Hey, Sherrie, look who's just come in.' Sherrie looked in the direction of Liz's pointing finger to a group of four people. Tim was one of them, and was pulling back a chair for a slim, elegant woman, whose dark hair was clipped back into her nape.

As if he could feel her gaze, he looked across the room, nodded and smiled.

'Who's that very sophisticated woman with him?'

'I don't know.' Sherrie picked up the menu and began to study it closely.

'I'm not very familiar with Greek food—can someone else choose for me?' This from a plaintive voice.

'I'd like feta cheese salad, dolmades, then some stifado.'

'I tell you what, why don't we have meze?'

'What's that?'

'You have all sorts of little bits and pieces and you can choose what you want. Saves a lot of worry about ordering.'

'Good idea, Liz.'

'Isn't that your boss over there, Anna? Is he very difficult?'

'Tim's not actually my boss. Ask Sherrie, not me. She sees far more of him than I do.'

'Oh, yes, tell us more. He's rather gorgeous, isn't he?'

'If you're looking for the Heathcliff type, crossed with a Greek god, I suppose he has a certain dark brooding charm. Not my type at all.'

'That's not what you told me!' Liz grinned. 'What was that comment about that lithe, rippling strength when he lifted you out of the trench?'

'Liz, you do exaggerate. I certainly didn't use a word like ''rippling''. I didn't mean anything by it.'

'I'll believe you...dozens wouldn't.'

The waiters hovered as the meal progressed. One in particular, with soulful brown eyes, was constantly at Sherrie's elbow.

'I think you've made a conquest,' whispered Liz, as he reappeared with yet another dish.

'You're always trying to pair me off,' Sherrie muttered. Finally they reached the stage of thick, sweet coffees and glasses of water. 'Does anyone want any halvah?'

'Whew, I couldn't eat another thing.'

'Nor me.'

'Nor me.'

'In that case, it's present time.' Anna stood at the head of the table and tapped for silence with a spoon.

A small table was placed at Kelly's side, loaded with gaily wrapped parcels.

'Kelly, these are just a few tokens of our good wishes, and we all hope you'll be very happy in your new life.'

'Thank you, girls.' Kelly sniffed and brushed a tear from her eyes, then tore off the paper, uttering small cries of delight as she opened each gift.

'Sherrie, that is absolutely lovely.' She held the crystal bowl in the air and they all gazed, entranced, as it sparkled and flashed in the candlelight.

'I was determined to buy something a bit luxurious, rather than the strictly utilitarian items on your list...' Her remaining words were drowned as a bouzouki and guitar started to play in one corner, the compelling rhythms drawing the waiters to the centre of the room.

In a line of six, with their arms resting on the next one's shoulders, they started to dance, stamping and turning as one. Bowing in acknowledgement of the tumultuous applause at the end of the first dance, after a whispered conference they hurried to Kelly's table and pulled the friends one by one onto the dance floor.

'Greek dancing is for men only,' protested Sherrie as she hurriedly slipped her foot back in her shoe.

'Not always,' murmured her partner, and Sherrie was soon caught up in the rhythms as the line moved past the remaining diners.

Smiling at her friends, Sherrie felt her partner

change and another hand seized hers on the right. Turning, she was startled to see Tim's smiling face a few inches from her own.

'What are you doing here?' she puffed.

'Same as you, enjoying the party mood and possibly making a fool of myself into the bargain.'

She watched him admiringly as they danced, noticing the easy movements of his body and how quickly he seemed to absorb the rhythm.

Just when Sherrie thought she couldn't carry on any longer in the strenuous circle, the music slowed and the guitar moved into a plaintive melody.

'May I?' Tim held out a hand as several couples left the circle, swaying and turning in time to the music.

'People don't dance like this any more, do they? Except on *Come Dancing*.'

'I do,' he murmured softly into her hair. His hand at her waist, he pulled her closer and rested his face against hers, and soon Sherrie was lost in the music, only conscious of the strength of Tim's body pressed to her and the sweep of his long legs as he steered her through the dance.

'What about your companions? Isn't it rather rude to just leave them, just sitting there?' Sherrie glanced up.

'Laura doesn't like dancing, she's quite happy to sit and watch. She knows how much I enjoy it and won't worry if I take a few turns round the floor.' He paused. 'And she is part Greek and enjoys the chance to sit and chat in Greek.'

Sherrie glanced across and sure enough, the dark-haired woman was talking animatedly and laughing with Sherrie's erstwhile admirer.

'What's your celebration in aid of?' Tim murmured.

'This is the hen-night I told you about.'

Tim tilted his head away from her and stared deep into her eyes. His own were amazing. Each time she met him they seemed to have a different glow about them. When he concentrated at work they were brooding, with injured patients a soft compassion shone through and when he laughed there was almost quicksilver in the depths of blue.

I wonder what they'd be like in moments of passion? The thought made her heart pound so loudly she thought he must hear. Suddenly the words broke from her.

'What colour eyes do you have?'

He smiled wryly. 'That's a funny question. Do you mean to say that I've been working in the department for several weeks now and you've never noticed? I'm quite hurt. And, anyway, what does it matter?'

'It doesn't matter. No, I didn't mean that. That sounds rude. It's just that you have such thick eyelashes, it's difficult to tell.'

'Depends on my mood. If I'm happy they're blue, if I'm depressed, grey, but watch out if they ever look green—that's when I'm losing my cool.'

'And what are they tonight?' She gazed intently at him.

'They must be blue. I'm really enjoying myself.'

He stared back just as intently. Almost in a dream, Sherrie followed her partner's lead and before long they were the only couple left dancing. She wasn't sure but she thought she felt a kiss touch her hair and heard a soft whisper, 'I could eat you.' Embarrassed, she pulled her hand free.

'I'd better get back to my table and I think you ought to as well.'

'Certainly, madam.' He bowed. 'I'm going now. Do come and be introduced. We'll be leaving in a minute.'

Uncertainly, Sherrie followed him from the dance floor and Laura stood and shook her hand. 'Laura, this is one of my work colleagues. Sherrie, I'd like you to meet my very dear friend. And Tom, and his wife, Jenny.'

'Nice to have met you,' Sherrie muttered, and hurried back to her own table. What an odd way to describe his relationship, Sherrie thought as she fielded questions from her curious friends.

'Right, who's won?' Liz produced a slip of paper, on which were written all the suggestions of what Tim's eye colour might be. 'Whoever said *yellow*?'

'Well, you know, like a panther. He moves like one.'

'We'd better make it three winners.' Sherrie grinned. 'He's got eyes that change colour according to his mood.'

'Rubbish,' Anna snorted. 'He keeps contact lenses in his pocket to make himself more mysterious.'

'Can you seriously imagine him doing anything as

vain as that?' Sherrie was amazed at the surge of annoyance that swept through her.

'All right. I was only joking.'

'I know. I didn't mean to jump down your throat. Blue, green or grey. Take your pick. What do you want to do now, Kelly?'

'I think a nice brandy all round to finish off the evening. I'll have to ring Jack to pick up the parcels. I certainly can't manage them tonight. Is it too early to think of leaving?'

'Not for me. I'm bushed.' Sherrie rubbed her eyes. 'And I've got another one of those extra emergency call-out duties in a few days.' Kelly raised a hand to the waiter and ordered. Swiftly he reappeared with a tray of drinks.

'It's very popular here, isn't it?' Sherrie glanced over her shoulder at the rapidly filling restaurant, where the waiters scurried to and fro. 'I don't think they'll be doing many more dances this evening with this crowd. That's a pity, that was one of the highlights.'

'We noticed.' Liz nodded knowingly.

Sipping from her glass, Sherrie studied the other diners, surprised at the momentary loss she felt at Tim's absence.

'Are you going to stay on at work after you're married?' She turned to Kelly.

The other woman nodded. 'Afraid so. I can't afford not to.'

'Wouldn't you miss it, anyway?'

'Of course, but there comes a time when you have

to let go, whether it's a relationship that's run its course or the end of the line for a job. I have been in ITU for five years.'

'I suppose that's one of the differences between us. We have to change every six or twelve months so we don't have time to get stale.'

'Everybody ready?' A waiter appeared at the table with an armful of coats and Sherrie took her black stole and flung it over her shoulder.

'What are we doing about paying?' Anna slipped on her bright yellow mac and pulled tightly at the belt. 'You don't pay, Kelly, this evening is on all of us.'

'I can't let you do that.'

'Yes, you can. That means we divide the bill into seven instead of eight.'

'Let me at least pay for the brandies.'

'Come on. We could be here all night, discussing it. I'll settle everything and you can all pay me later.' Looking at the rapidly forming queue, Sherrie pulled her credit card from her purse and passed it to the girl behind the desk as the others trooped upstairs.

'Are you sure? That's very good of you. I'll stay and keep you company.' Liz perched at the bottom step as the cashier handed Sherrie the print-out for signature.

'It's for my own peace of mind. I can't stand it when everybody starts adding up their section of the bill and counting out to the last penny what they owe. Let's go—the others will be wondering where we've got to.'

Quickly they ran up the small flight of stairs and into the street.

'Hey, rotten lot, where are they?' Sherrie stared at the deserted pavement, the light from a nearby shop window reflected in the pools of water lying in the road.

'Damn and blast, it's been raining again.' Liz pulled a scarf over her head.

'Surely they haven't left us here?' Nervously Sherrie stared into the shadows, then gasped as a tall figure loomed out of a nearby doorway.

'I don't know what you want but I should warn you I've trained in self-defence.' Quickly she seized Liz's hand as they both backed against the wall. 'Come on, back into the restaurant.' They pushed the door open with a crash.

'I'm going to scream in a minute,' Liz muttered as the figure came after them into the small foyer.

'Sorry, it's me. I didn't mean to scare you.' Tim pulled his jacket collar down from his face. 'The taxi was a bit full, and as I'm going back to the hospital, anyway, I was waiting to see if you'd like a lift.'

'We weren't scared, but I think you might have said who you were a bit sooner,' Sherrie said through gritted teeth. 'Of all the ridiculous things to do. Don't bother about the lift, we'll get another taxi.'

'They're very busy tonight—that's why the others crammed together in one and I said I would wait for you.'

Ignoring him, Sherrie picked up the telephone on the reception desk and called the taxi company.

'They'll be here in ten minutes,' she told Liz as they sank down into two armchairs. There was an uncomfortable silence. 'You might as well go on, Tim. We'll be fine.'

'It must be something in the air, all the women getting contrary. First of all Laura, and now you. What happens if the taxi doesn't get here?'

'We'll try another firm.' She could hear the irritation rising in her voice and all the enjoyment of the evening had dissipated in a moment. Cheek! Contrary women, indeed. Not that it was really her concern, but it was no wonder Laura had been upset, Tim not even bothering to take her home. Had there been some sort of argument? Well, she had no wish to be involved in any trouble.

Liz fidgeted and pulled back the edge of her sleeve. 'They're taking their time, aren't they?'

'I'm sure we won't have to wait much longer.' If he smirks or says a word, Sherrie thought, I won't be able to hold my tongue.

'Dr Walker?' Slightly out of breath from his run up the stairs, the waiter stood in front of them. 'I am sorry, there is no taxi—not for a long time. Would you like to try another company?'

'What do you think, Liz?'

Liz nodded towards Tim, who smiled at them both.

'The offer is still available.'

'Oh, all right. Don't worry about the taxi.' She smiled sweetly at the waiter, tossed one end of her stole more securely over her shoulder and walked to the door as Tim held it back for herself and Liz.

'What was all that about?' Liz muttered under her breath as they waited for Tim to bring the car round.

'Can't tell you now. I'll explain later.'

How could she explain it to Liz when she couldn't explain it to herself? Was she jealous of Laura? But why should she be? Tim was nothing to her except a professional colleague.

'Here we are.' Tim held open the rear door for them to climb inside. 'Or would one of you rather sit in the front?'

'No, we prefer it here,' said Sherrie.

'Home, James,' Liz said with a giggle as the car purred away from the kerb. 'Better than any taxi, this is.' She smoothed a hand over the soft leather upholstery. Sherrie was silent, staring from the window, her thoughts in turmoil. If she dared to look up, Tim's reflection glanced back at her in the rear-view mirror, his expression puzzled, his eyes behind the glasses questioning. Apart from the rhythmic sound of the wipers, the journey through the rain-washed night passed in silence. Even the irrepressible Liz was lost for words and Sherrie's sigh of relief as they went through the hospital gates was audible throughout the vehicle.

'Thank you, thank you,' she and Liz said as Tim pulled up outside the doctors' quarters and they got out of the car. Calling a brief farewell into the air, Sherrie hurried inside without a backward glance.

'Hey, wait for me,' Liz grumbled as she followed Sherrie into the common-room. 'What are you so up-tight about, anyway?'

'Nothing, just tired. Coffee? Or I've got some herbal tea bags in my room.'

'I'll stick to caffeine.' Liz spooned granules into two mugs. 'Coffee for you, Dr O'Neill?' she called across the room.

Sherrie turned slowly on her heel, not realizing Tim had followed them.

'Not for me, thank you. Just a glass of milk if there's some there.' Not looking in Sherrie's direction, he opened the refrigerator door. 'Alleluia.' He pulled out a carton and poured milk into a glass.

Sherrie watched the long line of his throat as he tilted the glass and swallowed. Then he wiped his mouth with the back of his hand and nodded towards them. 'Goodnight again.' Despite herself, as he walked across the room, his almost cat-like grace held her gaze transfixed before he disappeared through the door.

'Another coffee?'

'No, thanks, Liz, I really am tired.'

'I should get to bed. I've got two consultant rounds in the morning and God knows how many bloods to do beforehand. Are you going to tell me what's going on?' Liz said softly.

'Nothing.'

'Don't be daft. You could have cut the air with a scalpel. Oh, well, I'll just sling these mugs in the dishwasher and follow you up.'

Pulling the strap of her handbag more firmly onto her shoulder, Sherrie hurried into the dimly lit corridor.

'Can I speak to you for a moment?'

Her heart thudding painfully, Sherrie started as Tim appeared at the bottom of the staircase.

'That's twice tonight you've made me jump,' she said accusingly.

'Sorry. I'm a little puzzled about what I might have done to upset you. They say never let the sun go down on your wrath and, though this isn't wrath, I would prefer to clear the air or I won't be able to sleep for wondering.'

'You haven't done anything to upset me.'

'But you said hardly a word on the drive home.'

'I'm tired, that's all. Now, please can I go?'

'If that's all it is… But I need one small forfeit,' he said teasingly, his smile a flash of white in the dusky light of the corridor.

Before she knew what was happening he had pulled her close. Quickly she closed her eyes as his head bent and his lips fastened on her mouth softly, sensuously, in a kiss that set her blood on fire and quickened her breathing. His breathing became more rapid, too, then abruptly he pushed her away and ruffled her hair.

'Sorry, I shouldn't have done that. Although I'll probably look in before I go, I'm away from tomorrow so probably won't see you for the next two days. Perhaps it's just as well. Still friends, I hope?' He gave a husky laugh.

'You still there, Sherrie?' Liz's curiosity echoed in her voice as she saw them, and they stepped apart guiltily.

'I'm going.' Seizing her stole, which had slipped

to the floor, Sherrie ran up the stairs without another word and slammed and locked her bedroom door behind her. She leaned against it as she tried to catch her breath.

'Damn you, Tim O'Neill, damn you, playing with my emotions like that. Even if I'm nothing to you, I can't tolerate it.' She trailed her finger uncertainly over her burning mouth, convinced she wouldn't sleep a wink. Perhaps it was just as well Tim was going away. She might have a chance to gather herself together before his return.

CHAPTER SIX

FUMBLING in the half-dark morning, Sherrie depressed the button on the alarm clock and sighed with relief as its shrill summons was silenced. Six-thirty! Too early to get up. She pulled the quilt higher over her head, trying to go back to sleep, but in vain. Eventually, she gave in, plumping up the pillows as she thought over the evening at the restaurant.

'What am I going to do?' she asked her reflection in the mirror, just visible from where she lay. 'Life would be much easier if Tim hadn't come on the scene. But he has, and I just have to live with the idea that I fancy him like mad but can't show how I feel, not only around him but to anyone else, particularly Liz. She doesn't miss a trick.'

Without betraying how she felt, it had been impossible to explain to Liz why she hadn't wanted the lift in Tim's car.

'Come on, enough introspection for one day,' she told herself sharply, jumping out of bed and heading for the shower. She set the jet at its fullest power and stood under it for several long minutes, enjoying the force of the water on her face. Once she'd briskly towelled herself dry she felt almost human enough to face the day's shift and, even more important, calm enough to face Tim, should he appear at work.

Pulling on her white coat over her shirt and cotton trousers, she hurried down the stairs to the doctors' dining room, which was nearly deserted. Two strong cups of coffee completed the waking-up process and Sherrie set out across the grounds and entered the hospital.

She glanced at her watch. It was still too early for work. She turned off onto the main corridor and made her way to Intensive Care. She'd been meaning to call in several times to see how Stan was progressing. She'd rung to enquire, but it would be nice to see him in person.

'Sure, go in,' said the nurse to Sherrie's enquiry. 'He should be able to go to the ward in the next day or so. You're all keen to follow up, aren't you? Dr O'Neill was in yesterday.'

Sherrie smiled noncommittally, then pulled back the curtain the nurse had indicated.

'Good morning. You won't remember me, but I was there at the time of the accident. I just called in to see how you are getting on. Making excellent progress, by the look of you.'

Propped up in bed, Stan gave a lopsided grin.

'I do remember quite a lot, but it's not something I want to dwell on. I'm afraid I don't remember you.' He shifted on his pillows. 'I just know that I'm lucky to be here.'

'That's true.' Sherrie smiled. 'You must be very tough. Anyway, it's lovely to see you getting on so well.' She perched on a chair beside the bed and leaned forward. Stan seemed pleased at the company and chatted quite happily for the short time Sherrie stayed.

'I must go now but, if you don't mind, I'd like to visit again. Working in the accident department means we very rarely get the chance to see how our patients get on.' She shook his hand and glanced quickly at his chart, before leaving his bedside.

'Good morning.' The familiar voice stopped her in her tracks.

'Blast,' Sherrie muttered under her breath. 'Good morning, Dr O'Neill.' Annoyed at the fluttering of her heart at Tim's unexpected appearance, Sherrie surprised herself with the coolness of her voice. 'Just visiting Stan.' She moved quickly past him in the doorway with her head bowed, not wanting to meet his gaze.

'Two minds, then.' He said no more, just stood back to let her pass. A faint drift of aftershave reached her nostrils together with the smell of crisp cleanness from his newly showered skin that set her own skin prickling. She didn't look back but hurried outside and then to the accident department, enjoying the smell of the newly rained-upon ground.

Looks like a good start to the day, she thought, then grimaced as two ambulances drove past and pulled up with a squeal of brakes outside Casualty's main door. She went inside.

'Morning, Sherrie.' Mike, the other casualty officer, glanced up with a sigh of relief as Sherrie poked her head around the curtain of the cubicle. 'What a welcome sight!'

'Been a tough night, then, Mike?' Sherrie asked sympathetically.

'Well, there was a gap of about three hours from one till four so I managed to get some shut-eye. This is Mrs Jenkins, who has suffered an asthmatic attack. I'm waiting for the medical registrar to come and see her. Mrs Jenkins has had some aminophylline but it hasn't done much, as you can hear from her breathing.'

'Hello, Mrs Jenkins.' Gently Sherrie took the hand of the middle-aged woman on the stretcher, whose painful breathing had almost the intensity of a buzz-saw. 'Do you want me to take over, Mike, or shall I go and see the new arrivals?'

'New arrivals?' groaned Mike softly.

'Afraid so. Two ambulances, just as I came in.'

'Two? Oh, well, it makes more sense for you to deal with the new patients and I'll carry on here.'

Swinging her stethoscope lightly in her hand, Sherrie hurried to the main reception area as paramedics pushed two stretchers into the first available cubicles. A siren's wail, together with blue flashing lights which shone in the glass panels of the outside door, heralded the arrival of two policemen.

'What have we here?' Sherrie said softly to the first of the paramedics as she looked down at blood stains on the nightdress of the woman on the stretcher, who was sobbing quietly with her hand to her face.

'Mrs Baker. A row with her husband. I don't know all the details, but it finished with him using a knife.'

'Lovely!' Sherrie gulped. 'And who is the other one?'

'That's the husband.'

'What, him?' She stared disbelievingly at the mild-looking man, his thinning hair ruffled and his glasses askew as he peered short-sightedly at the ceiling. One eye was swollen and reddened.

The younger of the two policemen took off his cap and moved forward. 'Do you have any idea how long it will take to examine him? We'd like to interview them both.'

'I don't know how long we'll be. Perhaps you could wait over there. Get yourselves a cup of tea and, as soon as we can, we'll give you what information we can.'

'One of us ought to stay with him or, at any rate, just outside the cubicle.'

'Just outside,' Sherrie said firmly, and swished the curtain into place. 'Rob, can you give me a hand, please?'

Rob and Kate stepped forward, carefully slipping off Mrs Baker's nightdress.

'It's all right, Mrs Baker, don't get upset,' Sherrie murmured. 'This won't take too long.' She stood quietly as Kate sponged away the blood, revealing a cut about two inches in length just below the collar-bone.

'Anything more, Mrs Baker?'

'I don't think so, apart from the one in my stomach.'

'Stomach? Let's have a look at that straight away.'

Sherrie's eyes narrowed at the sight of the slash

across the stomach, which looked as though someone had plunged in a knife and pulled it towards him.

'Pulse and blood pressure are OK. Here we are.' Rob appeared with a trolley, carrying sterile bowls and swabs.

'Warm saline packs.' He pulled on sterile gloves and rapidly packed the injury with the warm swabs, stretching an Elastoplast dressing across to hold it in place.

'It's lucky he didn't go through the stomach wall completely, though this is bad enough.' Sherrie turned and smiled at the woman on the stretcher. 'You rest quietly. Are you more comfortable now? Good. Let's give her some diazepam, Rob—it might help with the shock—plus some ampicillin.' She scribbled the orders on Mrs Baker's chart and also checked whether she needed a tetanus shot. 'I'll go and see the assailant if Mike hasn't already done so.'

'Are there any other injuries?' Sherrie asked softly as she went to the next cubicle, where Mike was busy with an ophthalmoscope, looking into the seated man's eye.

'I'll tell you in a minute. Right, Mr Baker, apart from a nasty swelling, which will make your sight blurred for a few days, there doesn't seem to be any threat of lasting damage. Cover your good eye with this sheet of card and follow my finger with the other one.' Mike moved his finger steadily to and fro, and obediently Mr Baker watched him.

'You'll need to be seen by an eye specialist just to make sure, of course. How exactly did it happen?'

'I'd rather not say. It's between me and my wife.'

'We do need to know the way the injury was caused. It is a help in deciding on the best treatment. For the moment, I'll put in some soothing drops.'

'Mike?' Sherrie gestured towards the curtain. 'Can I have a word?'

'Sure. What is it?'

'Hadn't we better wait until either Tim or an ophthalmologist sees him before we prescribe anything? Especially in such a specialised field.'

'Come on, Sherrie, these drops are no more than artificial tears and that's what we're here for—front line. Wouldn't you prescribe plaster for a broken limb?'

'Yes, but that's a bit different—you can see the injury on the X-ray. With an eye, the damage isn't so apparent.'

'Sherrie, just because you are teacher's pet with our new consultant, don't question my professional judgement. Look yourself if you don't believe me.'

'I don't need to do that and well you know it. What a stupid comment and it's got nothing to do with what I'm saying.' She could hear her voice becoming shrill, aware of the warm colour staining her cheeks and the speculative looks from the two police officers. She breathed deeply.

'If Mrs Baker isn't too upset, I'll see if I can get more information from her. Has her husband been hurt anywhere else?' Sherrie said in a placatory tone. The last thing she wanted was to be at odds with any of her colleagues.

'He's got a knee injury—twisted it in a fall. Would you care to check on that as well?' Mike muttered, his expression grim.

'Is Tim coming in at all this morning? He said he was going away, but that he might look in before-hand,' Sherrie asked Rob in the next cubicle when she returned. 'If he has, I'll wait for him to see this lady before I call in the surgical team, but if not I'd better get on with it.'

'Better get on with it. He's not coming in at all today—a conference, I believe. It all falls on your shoulders once Mike has gone.'

Sherrie pulled a face. 'Did he give a number where he could be contacted?'

'Only in the direst of emergencies. But, don't fret, Sister is on early shift and so am I so you've got plenty of back-up.'

'I'll ring the surgical team now. I think they ought to see her, even though the wounds look pretty su-perficial.' She went to the phone and bleeped the reg-istrar's number.

'It was a good evening, wasn't it, Anna?' Sherrie paused at the reception desk during the first lull in a busy morning when time had seemed to fly past. To her relief, she'd managed to cope without Tim, even though there had been some difficulty in finding medi-cal beds. Now the department was nearly clear. Two more X-rays, waiting for the orthopaedic team, and she could grab some lunch.

'Kelly had a good time, which was the main thing,

wasn't it?' Swiftly, Anna flicked through patients treatment cards and stacked them in order.

'Do you ever play cards?' Sherrie laughed softly.

'No, why?'

'Just look at you sorting those.'

'Sherrie, are you busy?'

Rob appeared at her shoulder.

'For the first time this morning, no. What is it?'

'A four-year-old—walked into the path of a car. Just knocked to one side, but some nasty bruising.'

'I didn't hear an ambulance.'

'No, a good Samaritan brought the child in her car. Father's frantic. And so is the driver of the car. He's trying not to faint, I think.'

'Hope there aren't any spinal injuries. Lay her on a trolley and I'll see her now. And try and soothe the father if you can.'

Sherrie went to the child and stared down at the small body. One leg was twisted at an awkward angle and her white socks and small trainers were covered in mud.

'What's her name?'

'Mandy,' her father said huskily.

'Has she spoken at all? Mandy, Mandy, can you hear me?' Sherrie whispered gently in her ear.

Mandy whimpered and flung out an arm, then opened her eyes.

'Where's the person who brought her in?'

'I brought her. Is she going to be all right?'

'Has she been conscious at all?' Sherrie asked the middle-aged woman, pale-faced and shaking, who clutched her handbag tightly, unaware of the streaks of blood on the front of her jacket, and shook her head no.

'We'll get some X-rays. It looks at the moment as if one leg is broken but, of course, skull and spinal injuries are what we need to worry about. That's why we strap the head so firmly.' Sherrie pointed towards Mandy's head. 'To make sure there isn't any movement. Did she move her head at all?'

'No, I've done some first aid so I made sure I kept her head and neck straight when I lifted her.'

'Thank you. Get yourself some tea while we do the X-rays and I'll see if we need to ask you anything else.'

The two figures, father and rescuer, walked to the waiting room and perched side by side on the first available chairs.

Half an hour later, her spine showing no sign of injury and with just a possible hairline fracture at the base of the skull, Mandy was transferred to the children's ward under the care of the orthopaedic surgeons. The neurosurgeons were on their way.

'Mr Willets,' Sherrie explained, 'Mandy is going to the children's ward. Would you like to go so you're there when she wakes up?' He nodded eagerly and hurried towards the lift.

'Do you like kids?' Rob glanced up from the trolley he was cleaning, tossing swabs and gloves into a plastic waste bag.

'Yes, I suppose so. I haven't had all that much to do with children.'

'Tim was saying the other day how good you are with them, and I have to agree.'

'Oh, and when have you been discussing me with our leader?'

'Relax, he didn't say anything bad. It just came up in general conversation. No need to blush. We were talking about a major alert and the division of cases. That's all.' He pushed the trolley to one side.

'Now for a really tough job. To try and explain to that good lady that, though done with the best of intentions, it isn't a good idea to lift badly injured children and take them to hospital yourself.'

'Do you want me to do it?' Tim made his presence known behind her.

Startled at the sound of his voice, Sherrie spun on her heel. Annoyed with herself at the rush of emotion she felt, Sherrie's voice was ice-cold. 'No, thanks, I can manage. What are you doing here? I thought you were going away.'

'Change of plan. I gather I am still *persona non grata*,' he whispered softly in her ear as he passed. 'And I still have no idea what I've done to deserve it.' He glanced over his shoulder. 'Are you free this evening? Perhaps we could have a meal? I do want to try and find out what is wrong.'

'Aren't you supposed to be away? Anyway, I don't think it's a good idea,' she said stiffly, and walked to the next cubicle.

Tim seized her arm. 'Just a minute. For some reason you're annoyed with me or upset with me and I think it would be only polite if you told me what it's about.' He stared down at her, his expression noncommittal.

Uh-oh, she thought, his eyes look green so I'd better be careful. 'If I'm not held up here, I suppose I could manage a quick drink.'

'You don't sound too enthusiastic.' He frowned.

'Now I must get on.' Her heart beating fast, Sherrie hurried to the waiting area.

'I'm so sorry to have kept you so long. Have you had some tea? Good. I thought you might like to know that Mandy's injuries are not as serious as appeared at first.'

'That's good. I've a little granddaughter of about that age and it really turned my stomach to see her. I'll get along, then.'

'Could I just say one thing, Mrs Ward? I hope you won't be in any way upset. Mandy's father is extremely grateful for the way you cared for Mandy after the accident and would like your address to thank you himself. We're grateful as well—there are too few good Samaritans about nowadays—but it might be safer if such a thing happened again to call an ambulance straight away rather than carry the child in yourself.'

'I realise that now, but there wasn't a phone nearby and I didn't want to wait. All those hundreds of people that drive you mad with their mobile phones, and when you need such a thing there's no one in sight.'

'Always the way, isn't it? But thank you again.'

Sherrie shook Mrs Ward's hand then went outside. When she got to the cafeteria her earlier hunger had all but disappeared. Taking a bowl of soup and a roll to an empty table in the corner, it was all she could do to force down the soup, delicious though it was with vegetables in a rich chicken broth.

'There you are. I've been trying to get you all day. Is your bleeper working?'

Liz put her own heavily laden tray on the table and plonked herself down in the seat next to Sherrie. 'I couldn't quite understand all that electricity in the air last night between you and Tim. What was going on?'

Carefully, Sherrie brought a spoonful of liquid to her lips, before answering. The clatter of cutlery and voices in the background almost drowned her words as she spoke.

'I don't really know myself. I thought it was rather odd that he ditched his friends then latched onto us.'

'It wasn't odd at all—very kind, in fact.' Liz pushed back a strand of hair, before shaking salt and pepper over her salad. 'I'm supposed to be the dramatic one but I'm sure he didn't actually ditch them. It must have been simpler than that.'

'Such as?' Almost viciously, Sherrie buttered a piece of bread and pushed it into her mouth.

'Just what he said. He was coming back to the hospital, had room in his car and offered us a lift.'

Sherrie swivelled on her chair to face her friend. 'What would you think if your partner took you out, then left you to find your own way home, meanwhile picking up a couple of other women?'

'Sherrie, you're mad. We weren't picked up, as you call it. Anyway, how do you know Tim hadn't already arranged for what's-her-name to go home with the other couple because he knew he had to come back here? If you ask me, you're getting a bit hysterical over nothing. But I tell you what…' Liz swallowed a forkful of food '…I think he really likes you.'

'Don't be ridiculous.'

'I saw one or two of those looks he gave you last night. And I think you're pretty smitten as well.'

Hastily Sherrie got to her feet. 'I'm going to get some coffee. Do you want some?'

'Yes, please.' Liz giggled. 'It's no use running away. The facts are still there.'

'He's already spoken for, and with a little girl.'

Collecting the two coffees, Sherrie slowly walked back to the table. Was Liz right? Did Tim like her, as Liz had said? Well, the evening ahead would surely give her some indication.

Calm down, calm down, Sherrie said to herself. Amazed at her own excitement, she looked at the clothes scattered on the bed. What could she wear? She had absolutely nothing suitable for… For what? What did she think was going to happen? Gritting her teeth, she flung another skirt on the growing pile, telling herself she'd better decide soon because he'd be there in half an hour. Half an hour and she hadn't started her make-up. He sees you every day, including mornings when you look really rough after being awake all night at work, so try not to go too much over the top.

'Right, that's it,' she said loudly. 'That blouse al-

ways looks good and those trousers are plain or dressy
enough wherever we finish up.'

She quickly changed and then applied her make-
up—foundation, eye shadow and a slick of lip gloss—
before putting on plain pearl earrings and sandals. She
collected her handbag, some tissues and a credit card.

'Who is it?' Despite her keen anticipation for the
evening ahead, the rapping of knuckles on the door
seemed almost an echo of doom. The door slowly
opened and Liz's head appeared.

'Hey, where are you off to?' Chewing thoughtfully
at the end of her ballpoint, Liz studied her. 'I didn't
know you were going out tonight.'

'Nor did I until this morning. Liz, I'm sorry, I can't
stop to chat. I should have been ready ten minutes
ago.'

'Where are you going?'

'I'm not sure, out for a quick drink.'

'Oh, yes, and with whom, may I ask? Or do I need
to ask?'

'Please, Liz, I will tell you all tomorrow, I promise,' said Sherrie, as she saw Tim arrive.

'Good evening, Dr O'Neill,' said Liz. 'I didn't get
the chance to thank you properly last night, but thank
you for the lift home. Bye, Sherrie, see you tomorrow.'

Oh, God, was he here already? Hastily, Sherrie
pulled a brush through her hair, static crackling and
lifting the red-gold strands.

'Am I too early?' His hands tucked into the front

pockets of his stone-coloured trousers, the blue shirt emphasising the blue of his eyes, he studied her.

'No, I'm coming now.'

'Wow, look at that hair. No, don't tie it back, please, it's beautiful.'

'This sounds like the cue where the hero removes the heroine's glasses, frees the bun and says, "My God, you're lovely."' Sherrie giggled nervously. 'Except I don't wear glasses.'

'You're beautiful anyway. All set?'

He tucked her hand in the crook of his elbow and ushered her towards the stairs and out to the waiting car.

'Right, what is your fancy? Chinese, Italian or would a pub meal somewhere be enough. He looked across as she fastened her seat belt.

'Pub meal, please. I know a very nice place out on the Tiverton road, not too far, and their menu is more extensive than the proverbial ploughman's or ham and chips. Turn right at the T-junction out onto the bypass. Or we could take the scenic route if you prefer.'

'Let's live dangerously and take the scenic route, shall we?' He chuckled deep in his throat and Sherrie curled her hands in her lap at the sound.

'Before we start, I don't want to sound priggish but I'm not the sort of person who goes out with men already spoken for,' she said staring straight ahead as the road unrolled in the glare of the headlights. Before he could respond, she added quickly, 'Turn right at the roundabout—it should be signposted Bampton— then take the first left. Though we won't be able to see much, unfortunately, it runs along the Exe valley and is one of the most scenic roads around here.'

'If we can't see a lot perhaps we could try a visit again in the daylight if it's that beautiful.'

Sherrie remained silent, fluttering nervously inside as Tim spoke. He glanced at her, then skilfully manoeuvred the powerful car, following her directions. She stared at his hands, gripping the steering-wheel, fingers full of strength but fingers that could be amazingly gentle, as she had witnessed many times at work.

'Can you slow down a bit? It's not much further.' The road crested a steep hill and then curved round the bend. 'There it is.' Bright lights shone outside the inn, its sign swaying in the breath of air which had sprung up. Tim parked neatly on the slope at the rear of the building and opened the door for her. The breeze was cool after the heat of the car, enough to make her shiver as she alighted. She walked quickly with small steps, her heels rattling the gravel surface.

'No tripping again. I don't want to have to carry you in through the doors like last time. Can I ask why you wear such high heels?'

'You can ask, but I don't know if I want to tell you. It's because I'm short, of course. Why do you think?'

'I think you are the perfect height.'

'Oh, yes.' She laughed as Tim pushed back the door for her to precede him into the bar. 'And what height is that?'

'As high as my heart. What would you like to drink?'

'White wine spritzer, please.'

'I think I'll have the same. There's a vacant table. Sit down and I'll bring the drinks.'

Sherrie picked up the bar menu and went to the table, which was near a log fire, flickering attractively in the corner.

'Cheers.' Tim sipped at his glass, then placed the drinks on the table. 'Let's have a look at that menu, shall we? I must admit to being very hungry.'

He sat down next to her and, with their heads together, they studied the leather-bound folder. Sherrie could just smell the sharp, clean, lemon scent of Tim's aftershave, mixed with an occasional drift of wood smoke from the fire.

'Quite a selection. What do you fancy?'

'I can't quite make up my mind—something exotic, maybe, like crab au gratin or ham off the bone with a selection of salads. What about you? Whatever you have, try the bread—it's home-made every day and out of this world. On reflection, I think I'll go for the ham, with some home-made pickles.'

'I think I'll have the same.' Tim grinned, flicking the menu shut. 'And a few chips. There you are, we finish up with ham salad and chips in the end. I'll go and order.'

Sherrie watched him as he made his way to the bar. It was interesting to see the effect he had. Nearly all the female heads turned in his direction, with most looking hard and long. So it's not just me, she told herself. I don't know whether I'm pleased or sorry about that.

Their meal arrived very quickly and, to Sherrie's relief, it lived up to her expectations. The ham was pink and moist, the salads crisp and the chips piping hot.

'You're right about this bread,' Tim murmured, chewing busily. 'In fact, everything is great.' He leaned back with a sigh, contentment obvious in every line of his body.

'Would you like a sweet or a coffee?' Tim put his empty glass on the table between them.

'No, thanks. That was lovely but I couldn't eat another thing. You have one, if you want, or perhaps some cheese. I'm quite happy to sit here. It's very comfortable.'

'A very good choice of yours.' Tim bowed his head in her direction.

'It's one of my parents' favourite places. When the pub started to serve food the whole family would come here for Sunday lunch. That's when Dad could drag Mum away from the kitchen and himself away from the surgery.'

Tim was silent.

'What's the matter? Why are you looking at me like that, Tim? Have I a dab of sauce on my nose or something?'

'I was just thinking how lucky you are with your family. There are so few families like that now, aren't there?'

'I'm sure there must be loads. It's just that they're

not newsworthy and you don't hear about them. What about you? Are your parents still alive? And where did you grow up?'

'I went to boarding school in Surrey. My father did a lot of travelling and my mother went with him.'

'Are you an only child?' She put her elbows on the table and rested her chin on her hands, then wondered if he was being evasive when he asked, 'Are you sure you don't want a sweet or coffee here?'

'Quite sure, but please don't let me stop you,' she replied.

'I've had a much better idea. I make a very good cup of coffee. Come back to my place and we'll have one there. I promise to deliver you safely to the doctors' quarters at a civilised hour.'

'What about Laura? Wouldn't we disturb Amy?'

'No, we can have the place to ourselves. Laura has whisked Amy away for a short holiday before she starts properly at school.'

What do I do now? Sherrie wondered. If I say I'd rather not in case Laura wouldn't like the idea it looks as though I'm half expecting Tim to try something. And I'm not very sure I want to go back to his place. It's easier to forget his commitments if I can't picture them.

'We-ell, I'm not too sure.'

Tim placed his face close to hers. 'I promise you will be quite safe. It's getting very crowded here.'

Sherrie glanced over her shoulder. It was true. Most tables were now full and several couples seated at the bar gazed hopefully in their direction as the waiter cleared their plates.

'Oh, right. But I mustn't stay too late.' She laughed softly. 'I've got this boss who's such a slave-driver I'm scared to bits to upset him. He's a regular tyrant, I daren't be late in the morning. You see, he's a real superman and doesn't seem to need rest the way us normal mortals do.'

'Come on.' He took her arm and steered her outside through the nearly full bar area.

'Oh, not raining again.'

'Only a shower, and a light one.' They dashed for the car and Sherrie quickly buckled her seat belt, wondering what on earth she was doing—but it was too late to back out now.

CHAPTER SEVEN

WHAT am I doing? Her hands clasped in her lap, Sherrie sat as far from Tim as she could. The evening wasn't meant to end like this. She was trying to get some idea of how things lay between him and Laura. How she hoped to accomplish it in a cosy little twosome in his apartment she didn't know.

'Can I ask you something?' Annoyed with herself at the way her voice quavered, Sherrie stared fixedly from the window. 'It's extremely personal so I hope you won't take offence.'

'Be as personal as you like, Sherrie,' he murmured huskily.

'No, I'd better not.'

'Oh, that drives me mad. If you've got something to say spit it out. Don't dither. No? Oh, well.' The journey continued in silence, Sherrie nervous that whatever she said could be misconstrued. Tim said not a word, just whistled tunelessly to himself. 'Well, we're here now so perhaps you can ask me when we get indoors.'

They had pulled up outside an Edwardian house. The front garden was lit by a streetlamp, showing a well-cut lawn, but at the side and rear dark shadows of trees and shrubs were almost black, despite the bright lights of the car.

'Here we are—home sweet home.'

'Is all this yours? It's a bit big for just three, isn't it?'

'Well, it's four with Amy's nanny, of course. We only use the ground floor at present. I may let the other floors as flats eventually. You are right—it is big, especially as both Laura and I spend so little time at home. But I do like spacious rooms, and with this house I can have them. Follow me.'

He'd parked the car just inside a wrought-iron gate. Taking Sherrie's hand, he led her along the path to a covered area at the side. 'This way in. Let me take your coat, then go on through. I'll set the coffee bubbling.'

He switched on the light in a big old-fashioned kitchen to their left. Sherrie, not knowing what to expect, opened the white-painted door that led from a small hallway with dark wood stairs.

Tim reached behind her and flicked on amber-coloured wall-lights. After the sombre entrance and hallway the room was a shock of colour, and she paused in the doorway, dazzled. It was long, with its original high sash windows, but so light and bright that she blinked several times.

It was stark, yet somehow gave an impression of luxury. There were plain cream walls, a hearth of polished brick at the far end and two settees covered with jewel-bright colours, one blue, one flame, which faced each other. Nubbed linen covered the cushions. Brilliant abstract paintings, again in bright colours, hung between the windows.

'Wow, what a room,' she muttered a few minutes later as Tim came in with a small trolley, coffee-cups and percolator and a cut-glass decanter. 'Can I do anything?'

'Just sit down. Black with sugar, isn't it?' He poured the coffee, its rich aroma filling the room as he passed it to her with a small container of sugar.

'Brandy?' He lifted the decanter.

'Just a very small one.'

'Now, where did we get to?' He set his cup and brandy balloon on a small table and sat beside her. 'Just relax, Sherrie, you're as nervous as a kitten. I can sense it.'

'You're not wearing your glasses.'

'I'm short-sighted so don't need them for close work.'

Sherrie gulped. Close work? I'm torn in two. Thoughts scampered in her head like frantic mice. Part of me loves being here with him and part of me is terrified I might say something out of place. And it doesn't seem at all fair to Laura. Even if nothing happens. She put her cup down on the table and edged along the settee.

'To tell you the truth, I am nervous. I said earlier that I'm not the sort to go out with someone who is already spoken for. It doesn't seem honest to me.'

'Why did you come, then? Not that I'm not delighted you said yes. Anyway, what could be more civilised than a coffee and brandy with a friend? If I remember correctly, I was telling you about my family. Very boring stuff. I'm an only child—boarding school, as I said earlier, with my parents away most of the time. In the holidays I used to go to summer camps or on skiing trips arranged by the school so I saw little of them. More coffee?'

Sherrie held out her cup for a refill, picturing a small lonely boy, then thought of her own rumbustious childhood with her brothers and parents always around. What a difference. She'd been spoilt, but mostly with love. 'How on earth did you finish up...? Oh, sorry, forget I said that.'

'That's the second time you've done that,' he said. 'Finish what you were saying, for heaven's sake. Sugar?'

'Er, yes, please. I was going to say, how did you finish up the confident and successful person you are today?'

He leant forward and refilled both cups. 'Who says I'm confident?'

'Isn't it obvious? Just look at you, and it shows all the time at work.'

'Perhaps it's a big cover-up on my part.'

'So you're still a shy little boy at heart?'

'That might be taking it a bit far.' He laughed. 'Another brandy?'

'Whoa, no, thanks. Are you trying to get me drunk, Dr O'Neill?' Hastily, Sherrie covered the top of her glass with her hand and looked on nervously as Tim topped up his own glass.

'Of course not. What do you think I am?'

'Will you be all right to drive?' she ventured.

'Have no fear. I'll get you back all right.' He

tapped the back of her hand. 'Relax, I'm not about to attempt to force myself on you. I still haven't discovered why you were so distant yesterday evening and how I'd offended you.'

'We can discuss that later,' she said, hoping to avoid the issue altogether. 'Please go on with what you were saying.'

'You want to continue with my rather boring life history?'

'I don't find anyone boring. I love it at airports, watching everyone, or sitting on the bus and listening to the conversations around me. And I always feel a bit disappointed that we don't know more about the patients in A and E.' She straightened in her chair. 'Why did you become a doctor?'

'I don't know quite why I chose medicine. Perhaps because it's an occupation that closely allies you with people. It couldn't have been a better choice for me. I've never regretted it.' He was silent a moment, staring reflectively into his cup. 'And then, in my final year, the most important event ever in my life happened.'

He got up, wandered over to the hearth and returned with a framed photograph of a very pretty girl, her eyes slightly screwed up against the sun and laughing into the camera. 'It's always the way, isn't it? No hint. No one prepares you for it.'

'Prepares you for what?' Sherrie ventured gently.

'That lightning strike. Though with me it wasn't so much a lightning strike—more a blow to the solar plexus. Doesn't sound quite so romantic, does it? What the French call a *coup de foudre*.'

Tim was speaking so quietly she had to strain to hear the words.

She sipped her coffee then placed the cup into the saucer. 'I'm afraid I'm very confused. Do you mean Laura?'

'No, not Laura—my wife, Ruth.'

'Your wife? What wife? Are you married?' She sat back and looked away, unable to face the expression on Tim's face. 'I thought Laura was the woman in your life.'

'Sherrie, what I'm about to tell you is for you alone. I certainly don't want any sort of gossip or chit-chat at the hospital. You know how hospital gossip spreads like wildfire, losing and gaining embellishments on its way...' He put her cup on the table as Sherrie gazed at him, as if mesmerised, then took both her hands in his.

'I was widowed two years ago. Amy is the daughter of that marriage. My wife—God, I loved her so much—died of meningitis. I blame myself even now. I should have realised. I'm a doctor, for goodness' sake.' He ran his hands through his hair.

'There was a lot of flu at the time and that's what I thought it was. If it had been Amy with the symptoms, I'd have jumped on it straight away but you don't diagnose it quite so quickly with young adults, at least I didn't, even though they are the next most vulnerable group.' He picked up his brandy balloon and swirled the contents gently in his hand, then rose to his feet, wandered to the hearth and stood there, peering into his glass. 'She was dead in three days.'

'And Laura?' Sherrie said gently.

'I couldn't wish for a better friend. She was Ruth's closest friend and, luckily for us all, had spent a lot of time with Amy. She offered to take care of her until I'd sorted myself out and it's been like that since.'

Sherrie got up from the settee and stood beside him. 'Two years? But isn't she your partner?'

'Yes. Sorry, but I'm afraid that is a white lie. She has a nursing home and I'm her business partner so it is partly true.'

'My father always says that white lies are worse than normal ones because they are double lies. And doesn't Laura want a life of her own, anyway? Why on earth couldn't you just say you're a widower?'

'Oh, Sherrie, upright, Sherrie.' He leant forward and kissed her on the mouth. 'I'm not presenting myself as the greatest catch in the world, but there were a number of women who wanted to give me comfort, emotional and physical, and I just couldn't bear it. My only excuse is that at the time Laura offered me a way out and I took it. I'll get some fresh coffee.'

'No, I'd like to go. It's getting late. If I could use the phone, I'll order a taxi. I think your brandies may have you over the limit for driving.'

'You won't stay, then?' He held up his hands in front of him. 'No funny business, I promise. I have plenty of spare room.'

'Thank you for honouring me with your confidence

and cross my heart and hope to die.' She licked her finger and quickly drew a cross on the front of her blouse. 'I shan't divulge a word.'

Tim's smile was strained as he went to the phone in the corner of the room. 'Taxi on its way. I feel very uncomfortable about not driving you home.'

'Better not. Could I ask you something?'

'Uh-oh. Of course; ask away.'

'I still can't understand why your circumstances have to be such a deadly secret. Why did you tell *me*?'

'If you remember, when we first met you stated quite categorically that husband and children were not on the horizon for you.'

'So you felt you were safe from—what did you call it—offers of emotional and physical comfort, did you? I don't know if I am flattered or insulted.'

'Come here.' He pulled her into his arms. 'Yes, I did, but it wasn't only for that reason. It was also that you are so patently honest.'

Sherrie wasn't sure how the kiss started but, with his mouth on hers, Tim slowly walked her to the settee and pulled her down onto it. Gently he undid the buttons then slipped one hand inside her blouse, his fingers cool against her skin. His other hand caressed her nape. For a moment she was lost, her arms entwined around Tim's neck, her mouth opening under his.

Somewhere outside a door banged, jolting Sherrie back to reality.

'Tim, please.' Hastily straightening her clothes, she

pulled herself upright. 'I'm not sure this is such a good idea.'

'It feels like a wonderful idea to me. Sorry, I don't know what came over me.' He leaned back, his face inches from hers, and gently traced the outline of her cheek with his finger.

'Well, I do, of course. After Ruth, I never thought that such a thunderbolt could hit me again. I want you very badly. Ever since I saw you asleep in the office that night, looking so vulnerable, and then you were so feisty when I got to know you. It's an irresistible combination, almost as irresistible as that creamy skin and red hair.'

The shrill noise of the front doorbell came just in time. My God, talk about saved by the bell. Sherrie laughed nervously under her breath. Quickly she gathered up her bag and jacket and almost ran to the hallway.

'Goodnight, thank you for a very interesting evening.'

Tim opened the door and escorted her to the waiting taxi, then she turned and stared through the back window to see him lift his hand in a single wave, so she blew him a kiss in return.

CHAPTER EIGHT

DURING the short taxi ride back to the hospital Sherrie was completely silent, unable to concentrate on the driver's few attempts at conversation. He finally gave up. At least Tim hadn't already paid the fare. Fumbling in her purse for change and a tip gave her a few moments to collect her thoughts, before going into the doctors' residence.

Luckily the entranceway was empty and she ran to her room as though she could escape from all the ramifications of Tim's confession. She was very tempted not to answer the telephone call that came just as she got to bed, but training won and she picked up the receiver with a grudging hand.

'I just had to make sure you were back safely and to apologise if I embarrassed you this evening.'

'No. It was all right.' She wondered if Tim could detect the false brightness in her voice, but if he did he didn't want to discuss it. Before he hung up he merely murmured, 'Goodnight.'

She thumped her pillows into shape around her head, praying that sleep would come quickly.

Aware of how bleary-eyed she looked this morning after her restless sleep, Sherrie hurried past the reception desk in A and E, feeling almost shifty as she stared around to see if Tim was anywhere in sight. The thought of facing him after the previous evening was enough to set her heart pounding.

She muttered under her breath, 'It all seems stupidly complicated to me. After all, in two years you must have things sorted out in your mind by now.

'Morning, Anna.' She'd not been able to face even a cup of coffee at breakfast because her stomach had been in such turmoil so, with a quick glance at the list of waiting patients, she made the restroom her first port of call.

'I've just boiled the kettle. Tea or coffee?' Kate smiled.

'Coffee, please. I need something to wake me up.'

'You look a bit tired. Late night, was it?'

'Not really, but I had a job sleeping.' Sherrie took her mug and sat in the nearest chair, vigorously stirring her drink.

'Problems?' Kate asked sympathetically, buttering some toast.

'No, nothing important. No, thanks.' She shook her head in reply to Kate's wordless offer. 'No toast for me.'

'Hi.' The door flew back and Rob appeared.

'You'll smash the hinges one of these days.'

'I just like to make an entrance.' The charge nurse laughed. 'Have I got time for a swift coffee? One of the twins is teething.' He rubbed hands across his face. 'Sherrie, if you want to keep your girlish good looks don't have children, particularly twins. Come to think of it, I'm not being rude but you look a bit washed-out yourself this morning.'

'Let's hope it's not catching or we'll all crack up.'

She finished her coffee and rinsed out the cup. 'Here you are, Rob, have my seat. I'll just see what Mike is up to.'

She went back to the main casualty area, which even in her brief absence had filled rapidly. 'Hi, Mike, do you want some help here?'

'No, I think I've done for the moment. Just waiting for a replacement plaster.'

Sherrie looked at the little boy on the stretcher. 'Hello, Simon, what are you doing back again? I was hoping you were all finished with us.'

'One of the boys at school knocked into Simon and the original plaster was cracked. Unfortunately it shifted his wrist slightly out of line,' Mike replied. He picked up the case notes and went into the next cubicle. She followed him. 'I've checked the last X-ray with the orthopaedic team and they suggested another plaster, but for only two weeks this time.'

'Mike, please, you don't have to explain to me,' Sherrie said, horrified. 'You're not still on about that eye injury and the ophthalmologist I suggested, are you?'

'No, if I'm honest, it was a bit galling that you were right, but all is forgotten now and we're friends, eh?' He bent and kissed her firmly on the mouth.

'I like to see good staff relations but I think there is a time and place for everything, don't you?' Neither had heard Tim's approach, but the icy tone in his voice was enough to set her teeth on edge. He studied them both as they broke away from one another.

'I'll go back and see Simon. Do you mind, Mike? I saw him when he injured his arm the first time and I feel I know him and his mother a little. Good morning, Tim. Excuse me, please, I want to get past.' He stood back, his expression quizzical as Sherrie returned to the cubicle where Simon and his mother sat, waiting.

'All right, Simon?' Sherrie asked. The little boy nodded, supporting his injured arm and bravely forcing back tears. 'You'll have to make sure that if there is any trouble keep well away. That plaster is not meant to be a weapon, and you mustn't go around bashing everyone with it. It won't do the plaster any good and it certainly won't do your friends any good. What are you, a Power Ranger?' He giggled.

'And I'll get into terrible trouble with your teacher. Just be very careful from now on. All right?' She gently touched his face and left the cubicle.

There was a man with a leg injury who seemed to be asleep, one arm flung over his eyes, so Sherrie tiptoed from his stretcher and went to see the other waiting patients.

'My mates have all been on about my smelly feet. Sorry about them, Doctor.' Plainly embarrassed, the youth in overalls hitched himself up on his elbows and watched as Sherrie pulled back a sterile towel draped across his toes.

'For goodness' sake, don't worry about that. What happened?'

'I dropped a concrete block on my foot, and I swear my socks were clean on this morning but after only a couple of hours they get very dusty and smelly.'

'Ooh, nasty. The wound, not the state of cleanliness,' she added hastily as she studied the crushed toes. 'Don't you wear protective metal cap boots?

'Rob...?' She whispered in Rob's ear.

'Are you sure? Won't it embarrass him?'

'No, get the most flowery one you can find.'

When Rob returned with an aerosol can, Sherrie said, 'Here you are, save you worrying.' Sherrie held the spray aloft and squirted the fresh scent towards the ceiling. 'I can assure you, Pete, this is not for our benefit—there's no smell to worry us—but it might shut up your mates. Lie back and try to relax. Is it very painful?'

'Yes.'

'I'll get you something for the pain. Are you up to date with your tetanus boosters? You should be, in your job.' After he nodded, she said, 'We'll give you a top-up as well, just in case.' She wrote the prescriptions on the chart and handed it to Rob when he returned.

'I don't think I'm capable of that suturing, Rob. Is Tim around, or perhaps one of the orthopaedic team could have a look? It ought to be X-rayed, anyway. It must be agony. I've written up some morphine.'

'Do you want me to get hold of Tim?'

'If you don't mind. I'll see to that other leg injury, James Foster, if there's nothing more urgent on the agenda.'

'Not as far as I know.'

Draping her stethoscope round her neck, Sherrie hurried to cubicle six and pulled back the curtain. On the stretcher lay a young man clad in a denim jacket, a sheet covering his lower half. His jeans had been cut away on each side seam and around his left calf he had a heavily blood-stained bandage and dressing.

He raised his head from the pillow. 'Are you the doctor?'

'Yes.'

'Whew, things are looking up.' He winked and smiled but the effort of holding up his head was too much and he let it fall back onto the pillow. 'God, I feel dizzy.'

'Well, just lie still. It looks as though you might have lost a lot of blood.'

Sherrie watched as Rob carefully peeled back the bandage and a bright red spurt of blood flowed onto the sterile towel underneath.

'Looks like arterial. Let's have a suture trolley, complete with some arterial forceps,' Sherrie murmured. Quickly she snapped on latex gloves and pressed her thumb onto the cut at the bleeding point.

'How did you do this?'

Her patient grimaced.

'I'm stripping down an old car, a Morgan, and as I scrambled past it I caught my leg on the wing. I more or less ripped my leg away to get clear. The cut didn't look too bad at first. Until I tried to walk, that is, and more or less fell over, with blood pouring down my leg.'

Sherrie picked up the tray with the stitching equipment. For a leg she'd need a slightly stronger nylon.

When she'd completed that job, she told Rob, 'I'll see the woman in cubicle four, the acute abdomen.'

After going through the curtain, Sherrie said, 'Good morning, Mrs Hencliff, is it? I'm the duty doctor and I've come to examine your tummy. How long have you had the pain?'

'It started this morning before I got up.' The middle-aged woman, whose breaths coming in shallow gasps, her grey hair clinging damply to her forehead, was obviously distressed. Gently Sherrie peeled back the covering sheet and looked down. Quite a lot of guarding, all the muscles held rigid.

'I'm going to press gently to see if I can feel anything. Can you show me exactly where the pain is? Point with one finger.' Briskly rubbing her hands together to warm them, Sherrie placed them carefully on the woman's stomach and palpated the whole area. The patient's skin was clammy and the slightest pressure made her gasp.

'Have you ever had a pain like this before? Any vomiting or diarrhoea?' Mrs Hencliff shook her head. 'We'll X-ray your abdomen and I'll get one of the surgical doctors to see you. I'm not sure exactly what it is—it could be one of several things.'

'Did you say "surgical doctor"? Is it serious? Does that mean I might have to have an operation?'

'Not necessarily. Is anyone with you?'

'My husband's outside. Please don't tell him anything yet. He's such a worrier and if it's—'

'I think we might have to admit you. You have a temperature and we need to find out the cause of the trouble.' Sherrie squeezed the anxious woman's hand. 'I'll tell him very gently, I promise, whatever it is.' Then she went to the phone.

'Mainly on the right, could be appendix, though there's no rebound and it seems severe for that, but the difficulty with breathing could mean a gall bladder infection, I suppose. No previous episodes so not irritable bowel syndrome. Temperature's thirty-nine point five. I've given her pethidine for the pain and started antibiotics.'

Sherrie replaced the receiver as the surgical registrar promised to come straight away. She took Mr Hencliff to sit with his wife as they waited.

Leaving them together, she returned to Kate. 'This is nice and quiet. I'll have time to write up my notes in a civilised manner.' Sherrie leaned on the edge of the desk.

'Shh, don't speak too soon,' Kate said abruptly, clearing soiled dressings and used syringes into the bin.

'I might risk another coffee. And perhaps some toast now.' Sherrie went to the staffroom and smothered a yawn. Her restless sleep of the previous night was rapidly catching up with her. She felt she'd been placed in a large container, which had been shaken so that the floor wasn't where it should be with regard to Tim, and everything was topsy-turvy.

'There I was,' she thought, 'accepting the fact that he is to all intents and purposes a married man, and now the situation is all upside down and I feel I don't even know him any more.' Alone in the staffroom, she stirred her coffee and went over again and again in her mind what Tim had told her. And, because of her promise, she couldn't even discuss it with anyone to try to make it clearer.

'Oh, phooey, damn the man. My original intentions were right all along. To hell with getting involved and settling down. But who said anything about settling down? I'll stick to the job in future.' But I do want him very badly. The thought sent a shock wave through her.

'I want doesn't always get.' She could hear her mother's words echo in her head. God, she'd been spoilt as a child, especially by Dad, but this was something even he couldn't get for her.

'Get your hands off me. I'm all right and I don't want any of you messing about with me. You don't fool me with your prissy faces and uniforms—you're as bad as the police.' The shouting came from near Reception and, with her heart beating fast, Sherrie hurried there.

She stopped in horror. About thirty men and women, dressed for the main part in well-worn duffle-coats and mud-covered trousers, filled the area. Some wore hats but others clasped blood-soaked bandages.

Uniformed police, some also bleeding, were struggling to hold one or two of the noisier elements of the group. The man who was shouting kept throwing punches at Rob as the latter tried to calm him down.

'Shut up!' Rob shouted. 'Look at your stomach. I'm only trying to help you.'

Everyone stared at the trail of blood that was pouring onto the floor from below the hem of his grubby cardigan.

'You've been stabbed. Didn't you feel it?'

'Pigs, using knives now, not truncheons.'

'What's going on?' Sherrie asked tremulously.

'It's the new bypass. The local peaceful protest seems to have been taken over by a rent-a-mob crew, and the police are trying to sort it out now. Don't laugh,' Kate said tight-lipped, 'quote, before it gets out of hand, unquote. Sister is treating it as a major alert, though hopefully there won't have to be too many admissions. She's calling in other staff.'

'Oh, well, into battle,' Sherrie murmured.

'Not quite the best way to express it,' Tim said behind her. 'Are you all right?'

'All right? Of course, why shouldn't I be?'

'I wondered if last night...' he said softly.

'Oh, don't worry about that. Your secret is safe with me, although I must confess I don't understand why it should have to be a secret. It all seems unnecessarily dramatic to me. Hadn't we better concentrate on this lot?'

She entered a cubicle to find that Rob and two care assistants had managed to subdue the stabbed patient and had persuaded him to lie down on a stretcher.

'Can you take his clothes off, please, Rob, so I can examine him?' Sherrie's hands shook slightly while she waited.

'I'll see to him.' Tim walked softly into the cubicle. Turning to the man, he said, 'Come on, don't be stupid. You're not doing yourself any good.'

'Who are you calling stupid?' The patient lashed out at Tim but the bleeding seemed to be affecting him for his speech was slower and slightly slurred.

'You, if we don't stop the bleeding what do you think is going to happen?' Without waiting for a reply, Tim quickly put on gloves and pulled away the blood-sodden T-shirt to reveal a three-inch cut by the right collarbone.

'Just missed the windpipe, by the look of him. Can you put some pressure on this until we get him X-rayed?'

'Better get the portable X-ray and a radiologist down here, I think.' Sister surveyed the scene. 'There are at least five heads, one neck and possibly an elbow, and it would be a lot quicker.' She turned away. 'Anna, do you want some help with the clerking?'

'I'm all right for the moment, thanks, Sister.'

'Cuts needing suturing in cubicle one, possible fractures cubicle four, and let's try to keep the protagonists apart if we can.'

'Which one should I be seeing?' Sherrie looked at the cards already written.

'Here you are.' Tim steered her to an empty cubicle. 'You stay there and deal with the walking wounded.' Even in that brief moment, the feel of his hands at her waist was enough to set her pulses racing. 'I'll get Steve to wait outside in case anything gets nasty, but I think they are running out of steam at last.'

Gratefully, Sherrie glanced up at the security guard, finding his crisp uniform reassuring. She'd never in her life had any dealings with violence and she was surprised at how upset she felt. It was a relief when the first patient—a policeman—came in, supporting one elbow with his other hand.

'Sit there and rest your arm on the trolley. Wriggle your fingers if you can. Where does that hurt?'

He gave a yelp of pain. 'It's like boiling water all down my arm.'

'Kate, can we have a sling here until he's X-rayed?' She turned back to the patient. 'Just wait there. We'll get to you as soon as we can.'

Moving to another patient, Sherrie asked, 'Any other cuts?' Sherrie took the none too clean handkerchief away from the woman's eyebrow. 'A couple of stitches should help that. Were you knocked out at all? No dizziness or sickness, no double vision? If you get anything like that see your own doctor immediately. Here is a reminder of what your family should look out for. All right?' She handed the woman the small instruction sheet.

Kate put some gauze and strapping across the cut and led the woman to another cubicle.

The next hour passed in a blur, with a broken collarbone, more cuts needing stitches and a twisted ankle but, from what Sherrie heard from Kate as they hurried through their list, there were few if any serious injuries.

'I feel almost shell-shocked.' Gratefully Sherrie sipped the coffee Kate brought her during the lull.

'I don't wish anyone any harm, but it certainly gets the old adrenalin going, doesn't it? I must admit, I quite enjoy it like that occasionally. I wonder who won the battle of the bypass? Oh, in here, sir.'

Sherrie glanced up at the patient ushered in by Kate.

'Just sit down a moment. Where have you been hurt?'

The man fell back onto the chair and tilted his head to show her a large swelling just above his collar.

'How did it happen? Did someone hit you there?' She could smell the alcohol on his breath as she bent closer. He swayed again. 'Kate, get some help and a stretcher.'

Quickly, Kate went out and reappeared with Rob and Tim close behind.

'What is it, Sherrie?'

'I'm not too happy about this man. Can we lift him onto the stretcher?'

'Hang on a minute. Let's have a look at him first. He's a bit floppy.' Tim frowned.

'Whew, I'm not surprised.' Rob turned his face away as he steadied the man.

'Put a mattress on the floor and lay him carefully on it. How did you hurt yourself, sir?' Tim asked, peering intently at him.

'He hasn't said a word,' Sherrie cut in.

'Did he get an admission card? Ask Reception and find out if anyone is with him,' Tim said crisply. 'In the meantime, don't move him more than you have to in case his cervical spine is injured.'

'He doesn't look like a down and out.' Sherrie frowned, studying the clean white shirt, suit and well-polished shoes. 'And, no offence to the protesters, he's a lot cleaner than most of them were.'

'Did you want me?' The X-ray technician pulled up outside the cubicle, the machine's wheels squeaking to a halt on the polished floor.

'Yes, please, cervical spine to include that swelling there, also base of skull,' said Tim. He turned to Sherrie. 'Any clue as to his identity?'

'I'll go and ask Anna.' Pulling her coat more firmly around her, Sherrie walked swiftly to the reception desk.

'Have you seen our mystery patient? Just wondered if you'd discovered his name. Did he come in with anyone?'

'I haven't got any details, I'm still catching up,' Anna said apologetically. 'He seemed to be in with the general crowd so Sister steered him in your direction. Is there anything wrong?'

'He won't give us any details and I think Tim is worried about an almighty lump on the back of his neck.'

'Now that we've quietened down a bit and I've got it more or less straight I'll see what I can find out from the police, but in the meantime, here's a card with a temporary number.'

'Thanks.' Sherrie returned to the cubicle, where the

radiologist was finishing a series of X-rays, and gave the card to Tim.

The man was now in a hospital gown.

Tim stared at the X-ray films. 'He'll have to be admitted to Intensive Care. I'll organise that. Sherrie, can you see if there are any other injuries?' He walked away.

'Wonder why he won't speak?' Sherrie stared thoughtfully at the man now resting on the stretcher. A careful examination revealed no more injuries, though he had no movement on his right side. She scribbled a few notes on the card and waited for Tim to return from Reception.

She took the patient's hand. 'Squeeze and let go.' Nothing. 'Can you press your foot against my hand, sir, as though you're trying to push down the accelerator of a car?' She glanced at Rob. Again there was no response.

'There's a bed available in ITU.' Tim handed them the envelope of films. 'Anything here?'

'Hang on a minute.' Sherrie finished looking in the man's eyes. Unequal pupils. Stroke? Or the result of the injury?

He pointed to his mouth then took her hand and drew on it with his forefinger.

'Can't you speak?' She leaned close and mouthed the words. His lopsided grin told her she'd hit the nail on the head. Then he pointed to his mouth again, and then his ear.

Again she bent close. 'Do you use sign language?' He nodded.

'Oh, don't nod, old chap,' Tim muttered behind her. 'And he can't sign now because he has a right-sided weakness, either from the blow to the head or from a stroke.'

'Or possibly both.'

'Well done, Supersleuth.' Tim grinned at her.

'Still don't know how he got here, though. I wonder if on the list of foreign language speakers there are some who sign?'

'I'll see to that,' Rob said.

'I'd like him transferred to Intensive Care as soon as possible. Any more patients waiting from this morning's fracas?' Sherrie shook her head. 'What I can't understand is how he got here.'

'Someone must have brought him and, seeing the crowd at the time, decided not to wait.'

'Talking of crowd, where is everybody?' Admiringly, Sherrie stared around the department. Two nurses were cleaning and restocking trolleys, another was putting clean sheets on the stretchers and the domestic was swooshing round with mop and bucket, rapidly removing all traces of blood. Two protesters were the only remaining patients waiting.

'I think everyone deserves a pat on the back. It's not only the problem of dealing with so many patients at once, it's also that quite a few were rather unpleasant.' Tim clapped his hands softly in approval.

'Nothing like turn-out time on a Saturday.' Rob grinned.

'If Sister will agree…' Tim gave her a beseeching

glance '…how about take-away pizzas for everyone—my treat, of course?'

'Very kind of you. That would go down very well.'

'Has anyone got a menu and telephone number? Come on, Sherrie, we'll do the honours.' He lightly grasped her arm and ushered her to his office.

'There you are, sit there. We want a good mix—how many are there of us? About ten.' He looked at the list. 'Two vegetarian, a ham and mushroom, pepperoni, tuna and anchovies. That should have something for everyone.'

He rang the order through, then leaned back in his chair. 'Well, this is a bonus I didn't expect. Dinner last night, lunch today—the only meal missing is breakfast.'

'I never eat breakfast,' Sherrie mumbled.

'Well, you should. We'll have to rectify that at a future date. What do you think you would prefer? The full works, heart attack on a plate, or a rather more subtle offering?'

'More subtle offering?' Sherrie gulped. 'Offering where?'

'At my place, of course. Let's see, porridge with whisky, honey and cream, like an atholl brose, then a choice of hot rolls and muffins.'

'No croissants?'

'If you want, but I think they're rather overrated, don't you? With a selection of preserves, Buck's Fizz—orange juice is pretty boring on its own—and freshly filtered coffee, Kenyan or Blue Mountain. How does that sound to you?'

'Absolutely delicious, but completely irrelevant as it's never going to happen.'

'Forgive the cliché, but never is a long time.' He reached out and took her hand. 'I love your perfume.'

'I'm not wearing any cologne.'

'I know, that's what I love—it's a fresh, soapy, little-girl smell.'

'I wonder why Sister isn't called by her first name, like all the other staff.' Sherrie pulled her hand free. This whole conversation was moving rapidly into troubled waters and the sight of Sister's signature on the notice-board offered a lifeline.

'Either because it's something incredibly fancy or terribly unsuitable. Someone must know. We must try and find out. Those pizzas are taking their time, aren't they?' He leaned forward and straightened the papers on his desk.

'While we're waiting, there is something I would like to get clear,' Sherrie said. 'As far as I'm concerned, despite yesterday evening, you are a married man, well, the equivalent, shall we say? And I'm not interested in going out again, much as I enjoyed myself.'

He pulled his glasses forward on his nose and peered over them, grinning widely. 'I see. Did you really? Enjoy yourself?' And she had a very clear picture of how he would look in later years. Very endearing and still devastatingly attractive.

'You can't have it both ways. You don't want to be considered single so you can't expect dates.'

'No harm in going out as friends.'

'Sounds as though it's grub up,' she said quickly at the knock on the door.

'Lunch has arrived and, wouldn't you know it, another stream of customers.' Kate grimaced.

'Anything desperate?' Tim rose quickly from the chair.

'Not so far.'

'We'll have to sort out the ravenous staff from those who can wait. Come on.' With a hand at either girl's waist, he ushered them to Reception. 'We'll have to continue our discussion another time,' he murmured softly to Sherrie as they went to see the first of the waiting patients.

CHAPTER NINE

'Oh, what a beautiful morning,' Sherrie trilled, glancing over her shoulder to make sure no one was within earshot. The morning was lovely. A warm spring sun shone, burning away some drifts of high cloud. Birds almost drowned her voice as they answered one another from the lime trees at the perimeter fence.

'Someone sounds happy.' Rob came up behind her.

'Well, you have to admit, after all the rain we've had this is a big improvement.' Sherrie laughed. She gazed fondly at her friend. Of all the staff in the casualty department she found Rob the easiest to talk to, and if ever she had any uncertainty in what she was doing she only had to look to him for guidance.

'Experienced nursing staff are worth their weight in gold.' She remembered her father's words. Sister could be forbidding—in fact, it was easier to approach Tim himself. And despite all her efforts to be friendly with Mike, after his words about how Tim regarded her she couldn't help being self-conscious in his company.

'How long have you worked in A and E, Rob?' she asked as he held back the department door for her to go through.

'Too long, I sometimes think. I ought to push myself to get into something different, but it's so comfortable here. With a young family, you can't chase around the country in quite the same way as when you're single. I get a lot of responsibility as well, which I enjoy.'

Sherrie shrugged on her white coat. 'I have to admit, I'm still a bit scared that you have to make such instant decisions.'

'With the back-up of someone of Tim's calibre, you don't have to worry too much. Has he ever told you about his time in America?'

Sherrie shook her head.

'You should get him to. If you think this can be scary it's a peaceful stroll, compared with that. Do you know the highest cause of death there among pregnant women?'

'Haemorrhage, eclampsia?'

'Gunshot wounds.'

'Never.' Sherrie stared, wide eyed. As they walked through to Reception she added, 'Let's get on with our lacerations and sprained ankles, shall we? Possibly a bit boring, but easier to cope with.'

'Good morning, Anna.' Quickly she took the cards from the slot and began to go through them. Quite a few waiting, she thought. Never mind, Tim should be along shortly and just being in his company was enough to enhance the day. As though summoned by her thoughts, he appeared, his easy, long-legged stride swiftly covering the ground with little apparent effort.

'Good morning. I shall be busy in my office, if you think you can manage out here, Sherrie.'

'Of course.' She took the first of the cards from the list.

'Kate's on triage and we've nothing too serious so far,' Anna informed her. 'One bleeder from a gashed leg, I think, in cubicle six but all right otherwise.'

'I'm on my way.'

'Sherrie, before you disappear, can I have a word with you?' Tim said.

Her heart was beating fast as she hurried to his side.

'Don't look so worried. I thought you would like to know that Stan Havard is being discharged from hospital today.'

'Stan Havard? Already? I only saw him yesterday and he didn't say anything.'

'Amazing, isn't it? Our friend from the trench. And his grateful wife left a token of her thanks. If you'd like to come to my office when you have the time I'll pass it on.'

'That was nice of her, but she didn't need to do that. The major work was in ITU and the ward.' She paused. 'I enjoyed myself the other night,' she said softly.

'Sherrie?' Kate's voice called.

'Right. Coming.'

'Couple of nasty lacerations need suturing, apparently.' Anna waved a card in the air. 'And also your admirer of the other day is here.'

Aware of Tim's quizzical gaze, Sherrie's face coloured. 'My admirer?'

'The man who ripped his leg… Here we are, James Foster.'

'He wasn't my admirer, silly.'

'Well, the first thing he asked as Rob took off the bandage was whether the gorgeous red-headed doctor was working today? If not, he'd come back another time when you were here.'

'Oh, him.' Sherrie laughed. 'I didn't know you meant him.'

'How many admirers have you got, then?'

'Thousands. I need a computer to keep track. How do you do that?'

'How do I do what?' Anna stared at her.

'Keep talking and still rattle away on that keyboard.'

'It's my job. I could just as well say to you, "How do you do that?" when you're stitching up someone's wound. Phew.' Anna wrinkled her nose.

'Talking of suturing, I'd better see them now.' As she said this, Rob reappeared with the trolley, closely followed by Tim.

'Are you quite happy about this one, Sherrie?'

'Have a look and see what you think. It all seems to have dried out beautifully—quite safe to suture now.'

'Quite right. You're a very lucky young man.' Tim patted James Foster's shoulder. 'It could have become very nasty.'

As Tim walked out, Sherrie muttered under her breath. Young man! He must be all of six months younger than you. But she had to admit there was such a cheeky expression on their patient's face that he could have been several years younger.

'Jim, or is it James?' Sherrie rested a hand on her patient's shoulder. 'You'll have to rest. Is there anyone at home who can take care of you? You shouldn't put any weight on your leg until we see you again.'

'What are you doing when you've finished here?' James gazed at her with soulful eyes.

'Not looking after you, if that's what you're hinting. I'm sorry, there'll be no going out on the town for quite some time. Now we've put the fresh bandage on you just have to have your injection.'

'Oh, no, not the needle.'

'Be quiet,' Sherrie said sharply, embarrassed at the sideways grins she was getting from Rob and aware that Tim was only next door.

'Just the antibiotic, and then you can go.'

'In my bottom or in the thigh? I'll be quiet if you do them in my behind for me.'

'He's all yours, Rob.' With a thankful sigh Sherrie went to the next patient, but she couldn't help a small grin to herself at the outrageousness of her patient.

The remaining lists cleared very quickly, and Tim soon disappeared to his office again. She wasn't sure if she was glad or sorry. Glad to be left to use her own judgement, but sorry not to have the joy—if that wasn't too strong a word—of being in Tim's company.

'How are we doing, Kate?' At the next lull, Sherrie called into the triage nurse's cubicle where Kate made assessments on which patients should be put to the head of the queue.

'Fine,' answered Kate, as she scribbled on the

medical card in front of her. 'Pull up a chair. At least this morning we haven't had anyone demanding to be seen in order of arrival, rather than in order of how bad the injury is.' Kate laughed.

'Except for that woman who had her false finger-nail stuck in her ear. She shouldn't have been trying to scratch it so far down. And it certainly killed the dynamic businesswoman image. Did you hear her? ''I have an urgent business appointment. I must be seen immediately.'' I must admit I felt a bit sorry for her in the end, trying to keep her bare finger covered.'

'I won't stop. I'll hear soon enough when the next avalanche arrives. We've been very short of ambu-lances this morning, haven't we? Quite a pleasant change. I must go to the loo then get some coffee—in that order.'

Sherrie smiled and hurried to the cloakroom and then the staffroom, which was empty now but smelt pleasantly of coffee brewing. She'd barely filled a mug and added sugar when the door swung back to admit Tim, clutching a clipboard to him.

'Wonderful.' He sniffed appreciatively. 'There's no smell quite like coffee, is there?'

'Except frying bacon and toast.' Sherrie smiled. 'That takes a bit of beating.'

'I have to agree with you. It doesn't have quite the same effect, breathing in the aroma from a bowl of muesli or crunchy nut flakes.'

Sherrie giggled.

'What's the joke?' Tim's eyes crinkled in a sym-pathetic smile. 'You've got a most infectious laugh.

It's a pity we don't have the opportunity to laugh more often in our job.'

'I was imagining the Victorians, inspecting their warming dishes and huge platters—looking forward to seeing kidney, bacon and mushrooms and being offered instead some flakes that had gone soggy from the steam. Not very funny, I know, but it tickled me. Maybe it's because I'm in a good mood today and everything seems amusing.'

'Anything I find amusing is severely dampened by these wretched files.' Tim pointed to the folders he'd placed on the small table in front of him. 'And why are you in a good mood?' Sherrie was silent, unable to think of an answer.

'Changing the subject to pleasanter things than my paperwork, is there Irish blood in your family?'

'Not that I know of. Why?' Sherrie settled herself more comfortably into her chair.

'Just your colouring—that rich red hair and creamy complexion.'

Sherrie could feel the 'creamy complexion' darken swiftly. 'What about you?' she countered. 'Irish name, dark hair and blue eyes, put in with a mucky finger.'

Tim laughed aloud. 'It's supposed to be a "sooty" finger, I believe. "Mucky" doesn't have quite the same ring. I'm glad to have the chance to talk to you.' He sipped thoughtfully.

She turned, startled, as the door flew back with a bang to reveal an anxious Rob. 'Could you come and see this patient, please, Tim?'

'I'll come.' Sherrie stepped through the door. 'Tim's got a lot of reports still to do.'

'No, if you don't mind, Sherrie, I think this is one for Tim.'

Bewildered and, if she was honest, slightly offended that Rob didn't trust her judgement, Sherrie sank back into the chair, tapping her fingers impatiently on the arm as the two men disappeared. The click-click of the clock soon set her teeth on edge. 'I'm going to see what it is,' she said aloud. She jumped up just as the door opened and Tim appeared.

'Right, what is this emergency that I'm not experienced enough to attend?'

'It's nothing like that.' Tim took her hand. 'Sit down. Rob was quite right to call me. Your father is the patient and Rob thought this was the kindest way to let you know.'

'What's the matter with him? Is it serious? Let me go.' She shook her arm free. Shivers, feeling like iced water, ran down her spine.

'He's had a massive heart attack—the anterior wall, as far as I can judge from the cardiogram. Unfortunately, he arrested, and I don't know how long it was before he was resuscitated. Luckily, your mother started the resuscitation. Must have taken some doing. She is some lady. Come on, try and gather yourself together, not only for him but for her as well.'

'Is my mother here? She'll need me. I'm all right.' Though her legs were trembling, Sherrie managed to push aside Tim's supporting arm as he led her to the resuscitation area.

'Hello, Dad.' She barely recognised the shrivelled old man on the stretcher. 'Old man' was right. The pillar of strength from her childhood days had disappeared completely.

'What do you think you're playing at?' she whispered, taking his hand in hers. 'If you wanted to see where I work I would have invited you. No need to check up on me like this.'

He managed a lopsided grin. 'I'm only sorry to have frightened your mother.'

Sherrie turned to Tim. 'I'd better go and see her. Where is she?'

'She's waiting for your brother to arrive.'

'Brothers,' Sherrie muttered under her breath. Sure enough, when she went through to Reception she could just see her mother, swamped as she was by three tall, rugged men.

'Are you all right, Mum?' She hugged her mother close, trying to ignore her trembling. She turned to her brothers. 'How did you all get here so quickly?'

'I think, between us, we've been stopped for speeding at least six times.'

'What do you want to do? I'll go and find out what's happening, then come back and tell you, shall I?'

'I want to go and sit with your father,' Sherrie's mother said crisply. Straightening her back, she walked with firm steps towards the cubicle.

'Cardiac arrest,' Sherrie muttered under her breath

as she went back to the main work area. How long for? And why wasn't their own emergency ambulance called out? At least they could have started the anti-clotting infusion straight away. She glanced up at the clock over the main door, before popping her head around the door of her father's cubicle.

'Are you OK?' she whispered, swallowing at the sight of her mother, firmly clasping her father's hand and stroking his hair back from his forehead.

'Yes, your nice Dr O'Neill has gone to get some more reports before Dad is admitted.'

'He's hardly *my* Dr O'Neill.' Sherrie forced a grin. 'I'll see if I can find him. Would you like me to get one of the boys to sit with you a minute?'

'No, I'm all right.'

Sherrie went to Reception. 'Is Tim here?'

'I think he went somewhere with your father's ECG. I'm ever so sorry about him.' Anna smiled sympathetically.

'Thank you, Anna.' Swiftly Sherrie went to the tri-age cubicle. 'Anything urgent waiting, Kate?'

'What are you doing here?' Kate scolded. 'Mike's been bleeped and is on his way to take over from you and Tim is sorting the few urgent cases, including your father.'

'Thanks. I'll get back to him, then.'

'I'm so sorry,' Kate said as Sherrie reached the door. 'It's the thing we all dread, isn't it? Someone close to us being brought in when we're at work.'

Swallowing the lump in her throat at everyone's expressions of sympathy, Sherrie went back through

the department, her footsteps quickening at the sight
of the flurry of activity at the resuscitation cubicle.

Tim's tall figure and dark head was immediately
visible as he directed the other staff, and she saw a
ventilator and defibrillator by the stretcher.

'Oh, no!' She raced the last few steps to the group,
her eyes scanning the screen above the bed area then
searching frantically for her mother.

'She's waiting with your brothers.' Tim, reading
her mind, momentarily glanced at her. 'You go with
her. I'll give you a call as soon as things are more
stable here.'

'Did he arrest again?' Sherrie quavered.

'Yes, but we've got him back. Now, off you go.'
He put his hand to the middle of her back and gently
pushed her away.

Her eyes blurred with unshed tears, Sherrie walked
into an empty cubicle.

'Come on, come on!' she told herself firmly. 'I
can't let Mum see me like this.' She pulled a handful
of tissues from a box on the shelf, trumpeted into
them, then ran cold water over her wrists and splashed
her face. Biting her lip against the tears that threatened
once more, she straightened her back. 'Now, you id-
iot. Dad is being taken care of, but Mum still needs
you. Pull yourself together.'

'Are you all right? Sorry, take that back, silly question.' Tim had pulled aside the curtain. 'Just to tell
you we've managed to resuscitate and Dr Walker is
on his way to Coronary Care. With a reasonable sinus
rhythm, I might add.'

'Thank you. I'll get back to him.'

'Come here,' Tim murmured softly. He reached towards her and tilted her chin with his finger. 'No more tears. You've got to be the brave one of the family.'

She breathed deeply. 'I'm all right, really I am. It was the shock of seeing all the resuscitation paraphernalia at the bedside…and I thought he'd gone.' She could feel tears slowly start to well up, and stared fixedly at the ceiling, trying to will them away.

'Oh, Sherrie, don't, please.' Tim pulled her close, and with a grateful sigh she let herself be enveloped in his arms, his warm familiar scent filling her nostrils. She sniffed.

He leaned back and looked down at her. With feather-light touches of his mouth he moved across her face with gentle kisses, brushing aside the tracks of her tears.

'Don't cry. I hate to see you cry and things are much better now, honestly.'

'I know. That's why I'm crying.' She laughed uncertainly. 'I'm mortified. There's my mother. I don't think I'm exaggerating to say it would end any life she has that's worth living if Dad died, and she's coping much better than I am.'

The next hour passed in a blur. The only way Sherrie could cope was to dissociate herself emotionally as far as possible from the fact it was her father.

There was reassurance in seeing the familiar routine—settling the patient into bed, connecting him to the heart monitor and ventilator, the competence of the nursing staff and last, but not least, Tim's presence. Although he'd handed the care to the cardiac team, just having him close by made Sherrie feel that nothing bad could happen.

Gently Sherrie took her mother's arm. 'Come on, Mum, we can go and wait outside.'

'Do you think he might die? I want to be with him if he goes.' Mary Walker seized Sherrie's hand in a vice-like grip.

'He's much more stable now. It should be safe for us to have a break. In fact, if he stays as he is they might even be able to get rid of the ventilator.'

Sherrie glanced at her mother as they reached the waiting area. 'Can you bear to tell me how it happened?'

'Nothing out of the ordinary. He got up as usual, made a list of patients to see after breakfast. He complained of feeling tired this morning, but he's been called out a lot lately...

'He went into his office so I decided to put in that rosebush that I've had hanging about for ages. There was a call for him so I went to find out why he hadn't answered. I found him, complaining about a pain, but I still didn't suspect anything. I could kick myself now. I know I trained a long time ago, but coronaries were still the same then as now.

'It wasn't until he slid to the floor, clutching his chest, that I realised. I dialled 999 and started CPR. It's lucky your father made sure I knew how to do it. That's something that wasn't really around when I trained.'

'Mum, you did work a little bit after Florence Nightingale's time.'

Her mother smiled. 'I know, but it's true. We never thought of resuscitation then.'

Now comes the worst part, the waiting, thought Sherrie, almost getting to her feet every time there was a noise from the other side of the door. When a young nurse, her blonde ponytail bobbing on her shoulders, appeared and nearly ran along the corridor Sherrie could barely catch her breath.

It was probably nothing to do with Dad. There are other sick people in there besides him. To her relief, at that point the lift doors clanked open and her brothers appeared.

'Any news?' David said anxiously.

'Not yet.'

'Is that usual?' Colin, the youngest of the trio and the only one not married, asked.

'Yes, sometimes it take a little while to get everything set up.'

'Not this long, surely? What do they need to do? I know we don't know much but Dad was already on life support…'

'They will tell us if he gets worse, won't they?'

With her own uncertainties weighing heavily on her, Sherrie found the need of her family for reassurance almost unbearable. Oh, Tim, I need you. As though he'd felt her longing, he came through the ward door, and it was all she could do not to throw herself into his arms. She chewed at her bottom lip and tried not to give way to tears, her imagination vividly picturing each stage of her father's care.

'Oh, here you are. That's good. We can bring you all up to date.' Smiling warmly, he shook hands all round, then sat beside Sherrie's mother. 'Normally, Dr Forrester would be here to tell you what is going on, but as I'm a friend of the family I asked if I could explain the situation. OK?' He raised his eyebrows as Mary nodded.

'Being members of a doctor's family—sorry, two-doctor family—you all have a pretty good idea of how potentially serious it is. I'm not going to insult you by talking down to you. There has been only one thrombosis, despite the second arrest in A and E. We're doing continuous electrograph readings now to get a more accurate picture. Mrs Walker?'

'Mary, please.'

'Mary, of course. Have you any idea how long John was unconscious?'

'Four minutes by the clock.'

His deep voice continued with answers to all their questions and Sherrie could sense the easing of tension. If only she could feel his arms around her and the slow thudding of his heart as he held her close. She pulled herself upright, aware that he'd stopped speaking and everyone was looking at her, waiting for an answer.

'What do you want to do, Mum?'

'I'll stay here, of course, at least until John is more stable.' She took a firm grip of her handbag. 'What about work for Sherrie?'

'No question of that.' Tim laughed gently. 'It would be most unfair to ask that you try to concentrate. Will you stay here with your mother? And please don't worry about A and E. We can easily cover there.'

'Not too easily, if you don't mind.'

It's not just me he bowls over, she thought, looking on as Tim chatted to her brothers. He even produced a small laugh from David.

'We'll see to everything. Just stay here as long as you want and we'll phone later.' David kissed his mother and sister. 'I've got my mobile, anyway.'

They moved off along the corridor, talking soberly, and disappeared into the lift.

'I'm going to see if someone can get tea organised and also see if you can go in now.' Tim got to his feet and stretched his arms above his head.

'I'd like to see him, please.'

'Mrs Walker?' A nurse beckoned from the door. Comforted by the sensation of Tim's supporting hand at her waist, Sherrie followed her mother into Coronary Care.

CHAPTER TEN

SHERRIE fidgeted in the chair, stiff from the long night's vigil. At her movement, her mother glanced at her, then both women looked at the sleeping man and the monitor above Dr Walker's bed. 'Beautifully steady, Mum,' Sherrie whispered reassuringly. 'Why don't you go and have a lie-down for an hour? I promise faithfully if there is any change at all I'll fetch you.'

Mary Walker shook her head. 'He likes me here,' she said softly. 'I can tell. Why don't you go? After all, you are the one who has to work. I can sleep all day if I need to.'

'Work is all taken care of, Tim's seen to that. I can stay off as long as I need.'

'Well, that's very good of him. He's very nice, isn't he?' Mary raised her eyebrows, their lightly pencilled lines emphasising the pallor of her face.

'Don't start getting any ideas,' Sherrie muttered. 'He has a partner and a delightful little girl, Amy, the one who took Ben's fancy so much at the fair.'

'Why on earth do they call themselves "partners" nowadays?' Mary grumbled. 'Sounds more like an estate agent or solicitor, rather than the person you want to spend the rest of your life with.' She brought her husband's hand to her mouth and gently kissed it.

'There's no answer to that. Perhaps some couples feel the need for a let-out clause.' For a moment Sherrie wondered if she should tell her mother the real situation, but a promise was a promise and she'd vowed to Tim she wouldn't say a word to anyone. Besides, if her mother had any idea that Tim was actually a widower...well! So, although she was so near the truth, Sherrie bit her tongue.

'Sounds more and more like a business arrangement,' said Mary. 'For better, for worse, till death do us part.' Tears glistened on her lashes as she realised what she'd said. They were the first tears Sherrie had seen her mother shed.

'I'll get us some tea. I won't be long but I must just stretch my legs, anyway.' Sherrie pressed tissues into her mother's hand then tiptoed from the sleeping ward, which was silent apart from an occasional groan or snore from another patient. The night nurse, bathed in a halo of light at the desk, smiled as Sherrie went past, then looked back at her reports.

It took only minutes for Sherrie to boil the kettle in the visitors' room and prepare a tray. She found a packet of unopened biscuits and set everything out, before tapping gently at the ward door and returning to her father's beside.

'Come on, Mum, it's all ready.'

Reluctantly, Mary Walker pulled herself upright, and went to the desk.

'We're just going to get some tea.'

'I'll call you straight away if he wakes. Won't do you any harm to have a break, and possibly to try and get some sleep at some stage. You might have to be here for a while yet so going without rest yourselves won't help Dr Walker or either of you.'

Sherrie nodded and both women went to the visitors' room, sinking thankfully into the comfortable armchairs once Sherrie had poured the tea.

'The universal panacea.' Her mother sipped gratefully. 'You can keep all your Valium and so forth. How do you think your father is looking now? His colour is better, I fancy.'

'Well, according to the ECG he's settled into a steady rhythm. As the drugs start to take effect it should keep him like that.'

'Thank goodness they've taken away that wretched ventilator. That tube, sticking from his mouth, made him look nothing like himself. And I hated it because he couldn't speak. Supposing he'd been in pain and couldn't tell us?'

'They would have known. If nothing else, this is certainly going to teach me a lot from the relatives' point of view.'

'I was told I might get some tea here.' The door swung back and Tim's head appeared in the gap. 'I came up to see how the patient is.' He picked up a mug and poured himself tea from the pot.

'Very civilised, tea in a pot rather than a swift dunk with a teabag on a string. That's something the Americans can't do to save their lives—make tea. But, then, they think that about us with coffee.' He stared at Sherrie above the rim of his cup. 'How are you coping, ladies?'

'The eternal phrase comes to mind.' Sherrie gave a half-laugh. '"As well as can be expected."'

'According to Dr Forrester, the extent of the damage to the heart muscle isn't as severe as you might expect, following a cardiac arrest. And the second arrest was probably caused by a run of fibrillation. That's when the heart runs off into a fluttering action so doesn't pump the blood around as it should. More tea?'

'No thank you.'

'I think I might. I've probably got a long night ahead of me and I find tea as much help as coffee in keeping me awake.'

No one could have appeared less tired, thought Sherrie. His eyes were bright and his easy movements as controlled as ever.

'Not the most attractive room in the world, is it?' He stared around at the dark green chairs, a small television in the corner and a side unit, with kettle and crockery above.

'I don't think anyone waiting here is too worried about the decor so it's not too important, is it?' Sherrie murmured.

'Pleasant surroundings are a help, whatever the situation. Studies have been done on how colour affects one's mood. It might be helpful to have light blue walls, for example, as blue is a soothing colour.'

'I don't know enough to discuss it.'

Sherrie's mother got to her feet. 'I'm going back to John. You stay here, Sherrie, and have a break.'

Quickly Sherrie jumped up. 'I'll go back to Dad,

you have the rest.' Gently she smoothed her mother's cheek. 'You're looking very pale, and I'm used to going without sleep, don't forget.'

'I'm sorry, my love, but I need for my own sake if nothing else to be with him. And he knows I'm there, despite being so sleepy.'

'I'll come, too.'

'Do as you're told.'

'Oh, Mum, you make me sound about ten years old.' Sherrie laughed.

'Yes, stubborn then and stubborn now. Never grown out of it.'

Becoming more and more embarrassed as Tim looked on with a half-smile on his face, Sherrie sat back in her chair. 'All right, but I'll be back there in half an hour.'

Mrs Walker closed the door softly behind her.

'I see.' Tim gave her a speculative glance. '''Stubborn then and stubborn now.'' Straight from the horse's mouth, if you'll pardon the phrase. Well, I could guess that for myself. Is that why you won't come out again? But we get on so well, and your family likes me, don't they?'

Oh, they certainly do that, thought Sherrie. Having felt sorry for him, with Laura and Amy still away, she'd invited him to her home for dinner one evening. It had turned out to be a great success. His whole-hearted appreciation of her mother's cooking and the easy conversation that had flowed between Tim and her father had made the evening pass all too quickly.

But most vivid was the memory of the passionate

goodnight kisses in the hall, setting her whole body on fire. She wouldn't dare to be alone with him again.

'You've made up your mind, and nothing will change that?'

'Oh, please, you know why I can't come out with you. I thought I'd made that perfectly clear.'

'It's as clear as mud. I like you and find you very attractive and I thought you might feel the same towards me so why not spend a little time together?'

'Mainly because your personal situation, to say the least of it, is rather confused.'

'It's not confused at all.'

'Well, it's confusing to me. Where does Laura stand? Are you free or not? And what do you hope to gain by our going out together?'

'What I'd really like, surely, is obvious.' He growled low in his throat then laughed softly.

'No chance. Please...' she raised her hand '...I can't face any intense discussion now.' She rested her head against the back of the chair and closed her eyes.

'I'm sorry. Pretty heartless of me to try to talk you into anything under these circumstances.'

'Don't worry, you won't talk me into anything I don't want.'

'Sherrie, marry me.'

'What did you say?'

'I want to take care of you.'

'What are you doing?' She sat up abruptly as he touched her face.

'Relax. Rest back again, and keep your eyes closed,' he murmured. Slowly, his fingers rotated against her skin, exerting a gentle pressure on either temple. 'Lean forward slightly.' His hands travelled to her nape and Sherrie could feel the tension gradually drain away as he continued to massage.

'That's much better. What magic fingers! I do feel more relaxed now.'

'Think about what I said, please, Sherrie. I meant it.'

'Isn't it usually supposed to be a question?'

'Perhaps. I'd better go.' He moved to the front of the chair and knelt in front of her. 'You look tired, understandably, so I won't worry you now but, please, think over what I said. Am I being too heartless bringing up the subject now?' He rested his elbows on her knees. 'I've been wanting to say it for some time.' He brought his face close to hers and gently kissed her lips.

'I can feel for you. Although your father is stable now, you had no idea of the outcome when he was admitted. Try to get some rest, and your mother as well. I'll call again in the morning, before going to A and E to see how the situation is.'

Light-footed as ever, he went through the door. Sherrie thought she'd never seen a man of his height and build move with such grace.

Stacking the cups neatly, she returned to her father's bedside. She spent the remainder of the night in a semi-doze, half sleeping, half waking, until six o'clock when the morning routine of the ward started with the appearance of a tea-trolley for the patients, who stirred into wakefulness—some very unwillingly, to judge by the grumbles.

'I think I'd be a bit grumpy if I were woken up at six,' Mrs Walker murmured across the bed to Sherrie.

'Perhaps they have a lot to get through before the day staff arrive—electrocardiographs, medicines, blood specimens, washes for those unable to wash themselves.'

'Better than my day.' Mrs Walker laughed softly. 'When I trained reveille was at four-thirty on the busy surgical wards and you had to go like crazy even then to get everything done in the time.'

'Ah, the good old days, eh, Mum? Do you ever think you'd like to be working in today's hospital world?'

'Parts I'd enjoy, but I think there's been such a drift away from basic nursing care, and there's so much more training and management, you never get a chance to take care of the patients, which is what it's all about when all is said and done. It's a different life altogether.' She glanced around her. 'Nurses taking bloods, recording ECGs—just look at it. Possibly more interesting, but we all loved our life.'

'Hello, love.' Dr Walker's deep croak seemed to come from the depths of him and was barely audible, but he managed a half-smile as his wife kissed his forehead. 'You been here all night?' He looked across the bed at the two women.

'Most of the night.'

'Very silly of you. Now go and get some rest as I

expect they'll be up to all sorts with me this morning and you might not get the chance to stay anyway.'

Sherrie breathed deeply. Her father sounded his normal self so the cardiac arrest hadn't lasted long enough for there to have been any brain damage. Thank God!

'Come on, Mum, we'll go home for a few hours, have some breakfast and a bath and come back later. I expect the boys would like to visit as well, and we don't want to tire Dad out, now do we?'

'Of course not. We'll see you later,' she murmured softly to her husband.

Turning at least three times on her way to the door, Mrs Walker finally left with Sherrie's encouraging arm around her.

When she looked back on the following two weeks, all Sherrie saw was a blur of visits to the hospital, finding a locum for her father's practice, supporting her mother, with highlights such as Dr Walker home for a weekend visit and the panic at home to get everything as her mother wanted it.

Underneath it all was Tim's bolt from the blue, churning at her insides. Whatever had he been thinking of? Had he meant it? He'd not mentioned anything again.

'Mum, if you don't calm down you'll be the next one with a heart attack.'

'I know, I know, I'm being silly, but it's got to be perfect.' Mary picked anxiously at a bowl of flowers on a side table, adjusting the blooms.

'You've done that three times this morning already,' Sherrie reprimanded her. 'For goodness' sake, sit down and I'll make you a cup of tea.'

'I wonder if Dr Forrester has said anything about retiring?'

'Now, he didn't actually say retirement, but to take things much more easily. If Linda, the locum, is interested in joining the practice full time, that could be the answer.

'No, Mum, I'm ever so sorry.' Sherrie shook her head. 'I know what you're going to say but it wouldn't work, Dad and me, but I'll be glad to help until he gets back on his feet. We have very different ideas on how it should be done. He'll have to give up the idea of always being available for calls for a start, perhaps with help from a deputising service.'

She filled and switched on the kettle, and in moments set the teapot and cups and saucers on the table in front of her mother. 'You sit in the armchair. Go on, I insist.' They sipped their tea but both got to their feet at the sound of the car, pulling up outside.

Looking very frail but with a face-splitting grin, showing his happiness, John, supported by David and Sherrie, stepped slowly into the house.

They manoeuvred their way to the kitchen and helped John to the big armchair, where he wriggled himself into its depths.

'Great to be home.' He patted the arm of the chair. 'Like an old friend this is, and it's good to see all you lot, not looking up from a hospital bed.'

'Tea's on, Dad. Get your breath back and then David and I'll leave you to have a chat with Mum.'

'Caroline sends her love and Ben is desperate to see Gramps. I won't stay too long now but I'll be able to pop back this evening for a short visit,' said David with a smile.

'Don't worry, son, you need to be with Caroline now the baby is so near. How is she?'

'Counting the minutes until delivery and convinced she is the biggest woman in the world. And, of course, we've actually had some really warm weather the last couple of weeks. Now, are you sure you'll be OK if I disappear?'

He bent and kissed his mother and sister then went through the door.

'Bye, David. I'm going upstairs, Mum. I'm determined to throw out some of those things I never wear and this seems like a good opportunity. Don't move or do anything without calling me first.'

'I'm sure all my patients who've had heart attacks don't go through all this rigmarole afterwards. Being treated like Dresden porcelain.'

'I bet they do. It's just that you don't know about it. Call me if you need me.' Sherrie glanced back as she left the kitchen. Already her mother had pulled an upright chair beside her husband and was sitting by him, his hand loosely clasped in hers.

Oh, if I ever do think of getting married I'd want it to be like that. None of these partner arrangements. Unbidden, a clear image of Tim came to her mind.

She folded another two sweatshirts and added them to the growing pile of clothes to be discarded.

'Sherrie, telephone.'

Quickly she ran downstairs at her mother's call.

'It sounds like Tim,' her mother said, with one hand over the mouthpiece of the phone.

Her heart pounding, Sherrie took the receiver.

'Hello?'

'Sherrie, it's Tim. I'm sure I'm being a pest. I hope I haven't called at a bad time. I only found out this morning when I went to see him that your father was booked for a home visit. I wondered if there is anything I can do.'

'I don't think so, Tim. Everything seems to be under control. Dad's loving every minute here at home and we've done all the practical things, like fixed a bed downstairs and so forth. And Mum is positively indecent.' She laughed softly. 'All starry-eyed in the kitchen as they sit there and hold hands.'

'They are an amazing couple, aren't they? Sherrie, would I be in the way if I called in briefly? I promise I won't intrude on the two lovebirds any longer than I have to.'

A hand clutched at her heart. 'Is there something wrong? I saw Dr Forrester yesterday and he is very pleased with Dad's progress.'

'There are a couple of details that have come to light on the latest electrocardiograph and he thought you would want to know about them straight away. I volunteered because it's kinder to tell you face to face, and also—' he lowered his voice '—I miss you and I want to see you.' He gave a self-deprecating laugh. 'Talk about self-centred. I'm not usually like that, but it seems an age since we've seen each other.'

Sherrie's heart started to beat even faster, whether from Tim's words or from the worry of what he had to say, she didn't know. She replaced the receiver, after agreeing to see him in an hour.

She glanced at her watch then tiptoed into the kitchen.

'Shh.' Mary raised a finger to her lips as Sherrie started to speak. John Walker was fast asleep, looking surprisingly comfortable, despite the way his head tilted to one side.

'Mum.' Sherrie beckoned her towards the hallway. 'Tim is coming over shortly—hope this is all right? He's got something to tell us about Dad's latest ECG findings.'

'Not bad news, is it?'

Sherrie took her mother's hand in hers. 'I shouldn't think so. Everything was going so well, and they wouldn't have encouraged a home visit if there were problems.'

Unless they found them after we'd gone. From the look in her mother's eyes, Sherrie could see that the same thought had struck her.

'Come on, relax and enjoy Dad being home. Don't start looking for worries when they're not really there.'

'You're right. I'll let Dad sleep a bit longer, then see about some lunch. Do you think Tim would like to stay as well?'

'I don't know. We can but ask him. I'll go on up-stairs and carry on with my tidying, if you don't want any help.'

'No, all under control.'

'On second thoughts, is Linda around? I might have a chat with her and see how the practice is going.'

'She was in the surgery. Between her and myself we are taking on a nurse-receptionist. It isn't fair to Linda to take over a new practice without any help, and if Dad gets well enough to go back to work we can present him with a *fait accompli*.'

Sherrie patted her mother on the arm, then pushed open the swing door that led to the extension and her father's surgery. Linda quickly rose from behind the desk and shook Sherrie's outstretched hand.

'Nice to see you. How is the patient? As you can see, all quiet here. I don't know if it's because I've cured everyone or if they're all waiting for your father to get back.' She laughed softly, smoothing back her thick blonde hair from her face.

'Dad's progressing, but not as well as I'd hoped.' Sherrie sank back onto an upright chair. 'In fact, someone is calling from the hospital now to bring us up to date.'

'The consultant?'

'No, he's the consultant on A and E but has taken us under his wing. I was working there when all this blew up. Tim O'Neill—very nice.'

'Tim O'Neill? I knew a Tim O'Neill a while ago. We were at the same hospital. His wife died from meningitis. Is that the same one?'

'Yes, tall and dark, about thirty.'

'That's him. A lot of us thought he would never recover from his wife's death. I've never seen anyone so devastated by grief in my life. Blamed himself. Lots were prepared to offer him comfort, including yours truly, but he didn't want to know. I shouldn't be gossiping like this about him. He would hate it if he knew. He was always a very private person.'

'Still is, but you can be sure I won't say a word. Hospital gossip isn't my line.' Sherrie laughed. 'God, what an awful prig I sound, don't I?'

'I don't usually talk about people so there's no need to worry that I might say something out of turn about any of the patients.'

'That's good. Dad is positively obsessive about patient confidentiality. Actually, you'll get a chance to see Tim. He's calling round shortly. If there's nothing I can help you with, I'll get back to see if Mum wants a hand.'

She hurried to the hall as the front doorbell sounded, wondering if she looked as much in turmoil as she felt. But Tim's obvious delight at seeing her and the way he swept her into his arms pushed away any worries she might have had on that score.

'I've missed you far more than I thought I would. I'm a bit scared at the way you've got under my skin.'

'Tim, what about Laura? Your personal life is in rather a muddle at present, isn't it?'

'All is sorted. Laura, at her own request, has gone to stay with relatives in Greece.'

'Where's Amy?'

'Amy is with her until it's time for school. How do you feel about Amy?'

'I find her a delightful little girl.'

'Anyway, enough about me. What about your father?'

'Come on through, Mum is getting lunch. We'll eat first then you can tell us what's going on.'

'Whatever that is it smells delicious.'

Tim greeted both Sherrie's parents, before pulling back a chair from the table for Sherrie and sitting himself in the next one to her.

Tim breathed in deeply. 'If that tastes half as good as it smells, we are in for a treat.'

'It's a stroganoff, but chicken not beef and *crème fraîche* not cream—all low fat, you see.'

Mary ladled out the food onto the plates. 'Rice or bread or both.' She pointed to the other dish and the basket of rolls. 'I wonder if Linda is free enough to join us.'

'I'll go and check.' Sherrie pushed back her chair and went to the surgery.

'Mum says are you joining us for some lunch?'

'I don't think you want me there.'

'Come on, don't be silly. She's cooked loads as usual so there's plenty for everyone, and you can see your old friend, Tim.'

'I'll just wash my hands.' Slipping off her white coat and tidying away the stethoscope, she followed Sherrie to the kitchen.

'Here's an old friend of yours, Tim.'

'I wouldn't say that,' Linda protested.

'Linda, lovely to see you.'

Despising herself as she did so, Sherrie watched them carefully as Tim pulled forward another chair. Somehow, from Linda's tone, she couldn't help wondering about Tim and Linda, but Tim was his usual courteous self, generally talking to everyone. His eyes were fixed on her father more than she would have liked, but Dad tucked into his lunch with obvious enjoyment and laughed and chatted, without appearing at all tired.

'Thank God for your mother's cooking,' he said eventually. 'I didn't get much to eat at all and what I had was, well, to put it politely, a bit tasteless.'

'Right, I think, if everyone has finished, I'll make some tea, but you'd better have a lie-down, Dad.' Sherrie filled the kettle and put it to boil. 'I'll clear away, Mum, you sort out Dad.'

Quickly she cleared the plates and put them to soak. She couldn't wait to hear what Tim had to say.

'Can I help?'

'No, we're fine, thanks, Linda.'

'Call me if you need any sort of help.' She held out her hand. 'It's been lovely seeing you again, Tim. And looking so well.'

'And you likewise,' he said with a grin. He bent and kissed her lightly on the cheek.

Impatiently Sherrie rattled cups and saucers onto the tray, and was pouring the tea as her mother returned from the other room. 'Here you are, Mum, sit

here. Sorry to be so abrupt, Tim, but what is this latest
news from Dr Forrester?'

'It's to do with that latest cardiac arrest.' He took
a spoonful of sugar and stirred his tea thoughtfully.
'There didn't seem to be any severe damage, but now
it looks as though there is some enlargement and
weakening of the muscle. It could have been happening for some time without any symptoms, except being rather tired and breathless.'

'The left ventricle, do you mean?' Sherrie swallowed from her cup. It was the most important part
of the heart, the part that did just about all the work.

'It means a very restricted lifestyle, living with care
and certainly giving up the practice.'

Mary's cup rattled against her saucer as she replaced it. 'So, to put it bluntly, he could go at any
time?'

'Possibly, but with proper care it doesn't have to
be just around the corner. How much you tell him is
up to you. It's a matter of trying to find a correct
balance between being frightened to move and having
some sort of life. But I'm sure he'll be sensible.
Sherrie...' he leant forward and took her hands in his
'...would you like me to go so that you can discuss
it amongst yourselves or can I help if I stay?'

'You go, Tim. You've been more than kind, but I
think this is something for the family. I'll contact my
brothers and tell them and then, when I come back to
the hospital tomorrow with Dad, I'll have a talk with
Dr Forrester. I'll see you out.'

In the hall he hugged her fiercely. 'I'm sorry I can't

take away this pain for you.' Gently he smoothed the skin beneath her eyes with his thumb. 'Such shadows. I just feel I want to take care of you for ever. I hope you'll let me.' He kissed the corner of her mouth.

Slowly she opened the front door and watched as he reluctantly walked down the path, turning two or three times to wave before shutting the gate behind him.

She took a deep breath and went back to the kitchen.

'I reckon this calls for another pot of tea.' Mary managed a grin as she refilled the kettle and put it to boil.

'Phone. I'll get it.' Slamming the door behind her, Sherrie dashed to answer it. Already its shrill summons was enough to set her heart beating fast. Don't be daft, she told herself sharply. Tim's told us all the news from the hospital and he can't possibly be ringing so soon.

'Hi, Sherrie, it's your big brother here.'

'David. Is everything all right?'

'More than all right, it's great. You're speaking to the proud father of a little girl, mother and daughter doing well. Another girl in the family—thought I must tell Mum and Dad.'

'I'll get Mum now. Hang on.'

'Mum, telephone for you.'

'For me?'

'Yes, go on, hurry up.'

Her mother's eyes were bright when she came back. 'A baby girl, nearly eight pounds. David was there at the birth, and they're calling her Joanna Mary after the two grandmothers.'

'That's lovely—something to celebrate after all.'

'And I'm not too sure that there might not be cause for further celebrations in the family before too long.' Her mother gave a sly smile.

'Oh, yes, and what would that be?'

'Don't play the innocent with me, madam. I don't care what Tim's relationship is supposed to be, but I've never seen a man more in love.'

'Don't be silly, Mum.'

'And he already seems like one of the family to me.' Cursing under her breath as she looked away, Sherrie could feel a blaze of tell-tale colour suffuse her cheeks.

EPILOGUE

THE sweet smell of roses and freesias wafted across the aisle as a breeze crept through the open doorway. Motes of dust, tinted red and blue by the altar window, danced in the stream of light. A whisper of conversation accompanied the soft runs of notes from the organ.

'Your hat looks terrific, Mum, and so do you.' David gave his mother's arm a reassuring squeeze. As he spoke the notes of the organ paused, then the glorious sounds of Beethoven rose to the rafters and heads turned towards the rear of the church.

Slowly the small procession moved towards the front and Tim and his best man stepped into the aisle. Tim pulled at his tie then glanced over his shoulder.

'Are you all right, Dad? You could have left it to one of the boys—I would have understood,' Sherrie whispered, holding firmly to her father's arm. She wasn't sure which of them needed the most support.

'I'm not letting anyone else escort my only daughter down the aisle,' he muttered from the side of his mouth.

The rector stepped forward and Sherrie relinquished her grip on her father to David's firm support, then looked up at Tim.

'Dearly beloved, we are gathered here today...'

The time-honoured words rolled over her and the rest of the ceremony passed almost in a dream. When it came to the exchange of rings she panicked for a moment as Tim had trouble, slipping her ring on her finger, but otherwise it was perfect.

The signing of the register followed, then outside for the photographs. A cheer rang out as Tim clasped her to him in a passionate kiss, and Sherrie could barely contain her happiness.

'Come here a moment.' Taking her hand, Tim hurried to the shelter of a nearby tree. 'I just want you to myself before we get tied up with the reception.'

'I'm rather relieved we kept it simple. Look.' Sherrie held out her shaking hand. 'I'm nervous enough as it is. Besides, we could hardly do otherwise, could we, with Dad?'

'He will be fine. I can feel it. The whole day has been—and is going to be—perfect.'

He drew her close and planted a series of small kisses on her face.

'Bride and groom here, please.' The impatient voice of the photographer suddenly impinged on Sherrie's consciousness.

'Come on. They're waiting for us.' She seized Tim's hand and raced across the grass, the soft ivory material of her skirt flying behind her.

'Come on, you two.'

As the photographer started to organise everyone Sherrie studied them all from the sidelines. Dad, after much protest, agreeing to use a chair. His obvious joy was enough to balance his growing weariness. Mum still hovering at his side. Thank you, God, for giving him some more time and so able to come to my wedding.

Amy and Ben, her little bridesmaid and pageboy, chattering nineteen to the dozen as they perched on a wall with their legs swinging. David and Caroline, proudly showing off the new arrival. Colin at Laura's side as he had been ever since she arrived—another family wedding? wondered Sherrie. Liz wearing an outrageous hat, actually with tears in her eyes.

And last, but by no means least, Tim. Her doubts were now completely gone, whatever had happened in his past—the death of a beloved wife and a partnership difficult to understand. He was the love she had dreamt of but never expected.

'Did you think we would make it?'

'I told you love would find a way,' Tim said smugly.

'You didn't say any such thing.' Sherrie laughed.

The photographer called them over. 'Right, sir and madam, I'm ready for you now.'

She took Tim's hand and they stood in the centre of the group.

'Did I say how much I love you?' Tim slipped off his glasses and handed them to his best man. 'I don't need these for close work,' he murmured in her ear. 'And over the next few weeks, if not for ever, it'll all be close work between you and me.'

MILLS & BOON®

Medical Romance™

COMING NEXT MONTH

'Twas The Night Before Christmas...

CAROL'S CHRISTMAS by Margaret Barker

Carol needed to talk to her husband, Euan, the new Casualty consultant. Did he *really* want the divorce to go through?

INSTANT FATHER CHRISTMAS by Josie Metcalfe

Midwife Livvy was so busy, she missed the signs of her own labour! Perhaps it had something to do with the unexpected arrival of her estranged husband, Daniel.

ONE MAGICAL KISS by Helen Shelton

Will persuaded Maggie to give him just one Christmas Eve kiss to put an end to his attempts to seduce her. But what a kiss!

MIRACLES AND MARRIAGE by Meredith Webber

Emma was wary. It was hard to take Patrick seriously in his Father Christmas outfit but when he kept mentioning marriage, it was even harder.

Available at most branches of WH Smith, Tesco, Asda, Martins, Borders and all good paperback bookshops

CHRISTMAS

Affairs

MORE THAN JUST KISSES UNDER THE MISTLETOE...

Enjoy three sparkling seasonal romances by your
favourite authors from

MILLS & BOON®
Presents™

HELEN BIANCHIN
For Anique, the season of goodwill has become...
The Seduction Season

SANDRA MARTON
Can Santa weave a spot of Christmas magic for Nick
and Holly in... *A Miracle on Christmas Eve?*

SHARON KENDRICK
Will Aleck and Clemmie have a... *Yuletide Reunion?*

MILLS & BOON®

Makes any time special™

Available from 6th November 1998

MILLS & BOON®

Next Month's Romance Titles

♡

Each month you can choose from a wide variety of romance novels from Mills & Boon®. Below are the new titles to look out for next month from the Presents™ and Enchanted™ series.

Presents™

PACIFIC HEAT	Anne Mather
THE BRIDAL BED	Helen Bianchin
THE YULETIDE CHILD	Charlotte Lamb
MISTLETOE MISTRESS	Helen Brooks
A CHRISTMAS SEDUCTION	Amanda Browning
THE THIRTY-DAY SEDUCTION	Kay Thorpe
FIANCÉE BY MISTAKE	Kate Walker
A NICE GIRL LIKE YOU	Alexandra Sellers

Enchanted™

FIANCÉ FOR CHRISTMAS	Catherine George
THE HUSBAND PROJECT	Leigh Michaels
COMING HOME FOR CHRISTMAS	Laura Martin
THE BACHELOR AND THE BABIES	Heather MacAllister
THE NUTCRACKER PRINCE	Rebecca Winters
FATHER BY MARRIAGE	Suzanne Carey
THE BILLIONAIRE'S BABY CHASE	Valerie Parv
ROMANTICS ANONYMOUS	Lauryn Chandler

On sale from 4th December 1998

H1 9811

Available at most branches of WH Smith, Tesco, Asda, Martins, Borders and all good paperback bookshops

Your Special Christmas Gift

Three romance novels from Mills & Boon® to
unwind with at your leisure—
and a luxurious Le Jardin bath gelée to pamper
you and gently wash your cares away.

for just £5.99

Featuring
Carole Mortimer—Married by Christmas
Betty Neels—A Winter Love Story
Jo Leigh—One Wicked Night

MILLS & BOON®

Makes your Christmas time special

Available from 23rd October 1998

4 FREE

books and a surprise gift!

We would like to take this opportunity to thank you for reading this Mills & Boon® book by offering you the chance to take FOUR more specially selected titles from the Medical Romance™ series absolutely FREE! We're also making this offer to introduce you to the benefits of the Reader Service™—

- ★ FREE home delivery
- ★ FREE gifts and competitions
- ★ FREE monthly Newsletter
- ★ Books available before they're in the shops
- ★ Exclusive Reader Service discounts

Accepting these FREE books and gift places you under no obligation to buy, you may cancel at any time, even after receiving your free shipment. Simply complete your details below and return the entire page to the address below. *You don't even need a stamp!*

YES! Please send me 4 free Medical Romance books and a surprise gift. I understand that unless you hear from me, I will receive 4 superb new titles every month for just £2.30 each, postage and packing free. I am under no obligation to purchase any books and may cancel my subscription at any time. The free books and gift will be mine to keep in any case.

M8YE

Ms/Mrs/Miss/Mr....................................Initials ....
BLOCK CAPITALS PLEASE

Surname ....

Address ....

....

....Postcode....................................

Send this whole page to:
THE READER SERVICE, FREEPOST, CROYDON, CR9 3WZ
(Eire readers please send coupon to: P.O. BOX 4546, DUBLIN 24.)